31 MINI
Mysteries

R.T. LAWTON

R. T. Lawton

Cover art and formatting services by
Michael Kliewer @ CopterGraphics

Copter
graphics®

31
MINI MYSTERIES
(solve it yourself)

CRIME SCENE   CR

IME SCENE

ME SCENE

R.T. Lawton

Table of Contents

COLD FACTS

F resh out of law school, ink barely dry on the diploma, Katelyn Moore quickly found herself in the middle of her first trial. Everyone in her new law firm claimed the pro bono case was a loser, and that the firm's senior partner had merely handed her the file as something to practice on. They would be watching to see how she handled herself in court ...and see how many mistakes she would make.

Katelyn adjusted her yellow legal pad for the tenth time and waited for the judge's order to continue. Regardless of how bad the case looked, she'd just have to see it through.

"Is the defense ready to cross examine the witness?" Katelyn glanced up at the judge. Now came the hard part. Her client, Tom Johnston, had no alibi, plus the D.A.'s Office had somehow come up with a credible eye witness to the theft.

"We are, your honor."

Katelyn walked to the podium and spread out her notes. She lifted her gaze to Walter Quigley, the young man seated in the witness chair.

"Mister Quigley, you've already identified my client, Mister Johnston, here in court. Where did you previously know him from?"

Quigley appeared relaxed as he spoke.

"He did some yard work for my mother, raking leaves, trimming bushes, that kind of thing. He lived down in the bad part of town, and I think he recently started overcharging us for his services."

"You live with your mother?"

"I do."

"And did you confront Mister Johnston as to the latest bill he submitted?"

"I did."

"What happened then?"

"I had Mother write a check for half the amount and told him that was all he was going to get."

"How did Mister Johnston accept your solution to the amount of money in dispute?"

"He grabbed the check, called me a name, and left."

Katelyn shuffled her notes.

"I believe the next time you said you saw Mister Johnston was in December, and it was snowing?"

"That's correct."

"Tell me about it."

Quigley leaned forward in his chair, both elbows resting on the top rail of the witness box.

"I came home from work and..."

"Excuse me," interrupted Katelyn, "you said earlier that you're a clerk in a music store?"

"That's right."

"Very well, continue."

"Anyway, I pulled up in the drive, got out of the car and opened the front door."

"You have a key?"

"Of course. Like I said before, I live there."

"Just you and your mother?"

"Yes."

"Go on."

"So, I walked into the house, immediately turned left into the study, and there he was."

"Who was?"

"Our yardman, Tom Johnston."

"Mister Quigley," inquired Katelyn, "I can't help noticing that you wear glasses. How good is your eyesight?"

"With these lenses, my vision is corrected to 20-20."

"And without those lenses?"

"Not very good."

"Did you have those glasses on at the time you entered the house?"

"Yes, I was wearing them when I stepped through the door. I was clearly able to see what Tom Johnston was doing."

"And what was he doing?"

"Stealing my mother's valuable paintings right off the wall. A Vega and two Dylan's. I don't know how much she paid for those three paintings, but it cost her several thousand dollars just to insure them."

Katelyn consulted a document.

"I see by the police report that you weren't able to stop the thief."

"That's right," replied Quigley, "he pushed me down and ran out the door."

"Did anyone else see the thief?"

"Not that I know of."

"Was your mother home at the time?"

"No, she was visiting my aunt out of town."

With her left forefinger, Katelyn pushed her own glasses farther up on her nose.

"Excuse me, Mister Quigley, but in order to cover all bases, I have to ask you. Did you by any chance slip on ice covering the sidewalk on your way in and bang your head?"

"I did not."

"Isn't it true there was snow on the ground, and that ice covered your sidewalk that day?"

"Yes, but I was wearing good rubber soled boots and had lots of traction. I did not slip and I did not bang my head. I saw what I saw, and it was Tom Johnston stealing my mother's paintings."

"Mister Quigley, just a few more questions. Since it was winter time, was the thief wearing a heavy coat?"

"He was."

"Yet I assume it was warm in your house?"

"Yes, Mother and I set the temperature gauge for the furnace rather high to keep out the chill."

"And was it very cold outside at this time?"

"It was."

"How cold?"

"I could see my breath, but what does that have to do with anything?"

"Your honor," said Katelyn, "would you please remind the witness he is here to answer questions, not to ask them."

"So noted," replied the judge. He then addressed a few words to Mr. Quigley before turning back to Katelyn and inquiring, "anything else with this witness?"

Katelyn studied her notes thoughtfully for a moment.

"No, your honor, but I would request a sidebar."

"Both attorneys will approach the bench," said the judge.

Katelyn was the last to step forward, but the first to speak, and she did it low enough that the jury couldn't hear her words.

"Your honor," she whispered, "I respectfully request a dismissal of all charges against my client."

"Preposterous," whispered back the prosecuting assistant district attorney, "our eyewitness has positively identified the defendant as being the thief.

"On what grounds do you request a dismissal?" asked the judge.

"I believe the prosecution's witness has perjured himself."

QUESTION: Why did Katelyn suspect Mister Quigley of lying?

SOLUTION: Anyone coming out of the cold weather and entering a very warm house would immediately have fogged glasses due to the drastic change in temperature. Quigley could not possibly have recognized the face of Tom Johnston or anyone else in his mother's residence that day without cleaning his glasses first.

AN OPEN AND SHUT CASE

"Once I figured that part out," said Inspector Jones as he stirred creamer into his afternoon coffee, "it became an open and shut case."

"What tipped you to the phony alibi?" inquired Corporal Davis. "Everything seemed fairly straight up to me."

"Let's recount the facts," Jones replied. "There were three workers, including the owner, at the small resort lodge this morning. Breakfast had already been served and all of the guests were headed out to the lake. It was only after the boat had engine trouble and wouldn't start that the guests returned to their rooms. Ten minutes in all. At that point, Mrs. Vasquez discovered her diamonds were missing from her suitcase."

"We had already established," the Corporal interjected, "there were no new arrivals at the resort that morning. Since all the guests were together on the boat dock when the diamonds were stolen, that pretty much left the owner and his two employees as main suspects for the theft."

"Correct," said Inspector Jones. "All we had to do to solve the crime was interview those three and see who didn't have a good alibi."

The Corporal appeared to think about the Inspector's last statement before continuing. "Well, we knew the employee named Ted, who worked as dishwasher and cleanup man, had a solid alibi during those ten minutes because we had him on tape. The lodge's security camera focused on the front door from inside the dining room showed him busing the tables and mopping the floor. Ted wasn't out of sight for more than a minute or two at any one time. Not absent long enough to have gone upstairs, into Mrs. Vasquez's room, taken her diamonds and returned to the dining room."

Corporal Davis paused for a moment to consult his notebook. "Therefore, I assumed the video eliminated Ted as a suspect, but that still left the owner and his other employee, Roger, the cook."

"Right again," said Inspector Jones.

"But those two gave an alibi for each other which seemed to match the picture hanging project they said they did in the small bathroom under the stairs."

"Let's look at their alibi again," replied Inspector Jones. "Roger the cook claimed he was inside the small bathroom hanging a picture centered on the wall to the left of the door when he saw the owner standing in the hall. The owner claimed that yes, he was outside in the hallway telling Roger that the three-foot wide picture and old wooden frame were too heavy to just hammer a nail in the wallboard and have it stay. They needed to drill a couple of holes and install solid anchors to hold all that weight."

"And they did," said the Corporal. "I went into the bathroom, closed the door and removed the picture to look for myself. Sure enough, there were two anchors installed in the left wall. That project had to take them at least ten minutes to do all that work, plus Roger complained the owner stayed in the hallway until the work was finished. Thus, they provided an alibi for each other."

"That's part of what I found interesting," said the Inspector. "Tell me, did you happen to measure the bathroom?"

"I did," replied Corporal Davis. "It was six foot by six foot, barely enough room to be called a half-bath. Why, what's wrong here?"

"Their alibis didn't hang together as well as that heavy picture on the wall when I finally thought about it," said Inspector Jones. "I knew one of those two had to be the thief and the other was the lookout. They must've hung the picture at an earlier time."

Question: What did Inspector Jones find wrong with the two men's mutual alibi.

Solution: A three-foot wide picture on the door's left would take up half the wall space. Even Corporal Davis closed the door in order to take the picture off the wall to see where anchors had been installed. But if the door had been closed as necessary for Roger to do the work of drilling and installing, then how could the two see each other, much less have the owner supervise the installation from the hallway?

CAUGHT IN THE TIDE

One of the few female officers in the Marine Patrol, Angel Smits felt she had to prove herself almost every day. And, as she grabbed for the constantly ringing telephone, it looked like this would be another one of those proving days.

"You've got noisy sea lions near your beach house?" Angel inquired into the phone. "Sorry ma'am, I'm the only one in the office. All the other officers are occupied with a problem in the harbor."

She listened patiently to the elderly lady on the other end of the line before replying.

"No ma'am, I don't know when they'll be free."

Angel glanced up as a man barged into her office and plopped himself into a chair on the other side of her desk.

"I need to report a homicide," he gasped, "on my sailboat, the Shady Lady."

Angel immediately promised to send the first available officer out to check on the lady's noisy sea lions, then hung up the phone.

"Let's start with your name, sir," she said to the man across the desk as she took out pen and notebook.

"Harry Wintworth," replied the man, "I'm Chief Financial Officer of Environ Enterprises."

"You've notified the police about the death?"

"No, I assumed the Marine Patrol had jurisdiction over boats offshore. I would've called you, but my cell phone battery went dead. So I drove here."

"Where's your boat located?"

"Anchored about three miles down the coast, in a large bay where the water usually stays flat and calm. It's rather private with only one dirt road coming in from the highway."

Angel scribbled notes.

"Tell me what happened."

"An investigative journalist by the name of Ronald Coe was doing a piece on corporate corruption for the Gazette. He called me this morning to request a private meeting. I guess he wanted me to confirm some information he had received about Environ Enterprises. We agreed to meet at my sailboat out in the bay."

"Go on."

"Unfortunately, he showed up a couple of hours early. At the time, I was still hiking up on the sea cliffs for exercise, too far away to get his attention. By the time I got back down to the beach, both he and the dinghy I'd used to come ashore were gone. When I looked out over the water, I saw my dinghy tied up to the Shady Lady. I tried shouting, but there was no visible activity onboard my sailboat."

"Continue."

"So I went out to the Shady Lady."

"How did you get there if your dinghy was already

10

gone from the beach?"

"Someone else must've showed up at the bay while I was climbing back down the cliffs because I found a small rubber raft pulled up above the high tide line on the sand. I took their raft and paddled out."

"Did you see anyone else?"

"No, but earlier I heard the sound of a vehicle leaving on the dirt road as I worked my way down to the beach."

Angel glanced up at Mr. Wintworth.

"Any other vehicles in the vicinity?"

"Just Ronald Coe's old white sedan that he drove out from town. I had to use his car in order to get here."

Angel paused to collect her thoughts.

"What exactly did you find on your sailboat?"

"Coe was lying on the floor of the cabin. He'd been killed with a shotgun, but the killer had obviously missed with his first shot because there was a fist-sized hole in the hull about two feet above the waterline. I checked Coe for a pulse, but it was too late."

Wintworth pulled a pack of cigarettes out of his sailing jacket. Angel quickly pointed to a NO SMOKING sign on the wall. He slid the pack back into his jacket.

"Anyway, I went through Coe's pockets," Wintworth continued, "and found his car keys. Searching a dead man sounds macabre, but his car was the only available transportation."

"Anything else?"

"Oh yeah, before I left, I jammed a thick stack of paper into the fist-sized hole to keep the ocean from pouring in."

"A wad of paper?" inquired Angel.

"It was all I could find at the moment," he explained.

"And since the tide rises about three feet or more about now in that bay, I didn't want my boat to sink before I could get back with proper supplies to make repairs."

"Plus," ventured Angel, "seawater might ruin any evidence at the crime scene".

"Well there is that too," replied Wintworth with a somber face. "Unfortunately, in my haste to plug the hole, the papers I used may have been the reporter's only notes from his investigation. I didn't realize what I'd done until I was almost here. At that point, it was too late to turn back, the tide had already risen and the documents would've been too soaked to be legible anyway."

"I'm sure you did the best you could under the circumstances," soothed Angel. "Now if you'll excuse me, I have to make a phone call to my supervisor."

Very carefully, Angel removed her automatic from the holster on her hip and placed the handgun on top of her desk. She kept her right hand on the pistol just in case she needed it in a hurry.

QUESTION: What made Angel suspect Mr. Wintworth may have been the killer?

SOLUTION: Even though the hole in the sailboat hull was two feet above the waterline with the tide rising three feet or more, it makes no difference. Since a boat floats on top of the water, it rises with the tide. Regardless how many feet the tide came up, the hole in the sailboat hull would still be two feet above the waterline. Therefore, if the documents stuffed in the hole were later found to be water-damaged, as Wintworth suggested they would be, then it was because Wintworth had soaked them first to ensure that the discovered evidence of financial corruption on his part was now unreadable

IT DIDN'T ADD UP

D etective Francine Caldera, better known as Frankie to her fellow vice cops, asked to hear the story one more time from the beginning. "Whatever you want," replied the big man sitting on the other side of the grey metal table in the interview room. "Just hurry up and catch those two guys before something bad happens to my boss."

Frankie turned on the tape recorder. "Start with your name and occupation."

"Jerry Landreth," said the big man. "I'm a chauffeur and bodyguard for Mister Johnston. He's the CEO for a large manufacturing company and a very wealthy and influential man here in town."

Frankie motioned for him to continue.

"I was driving Mister Johnston from his house to the manufacturing plant just like I do five days out of every week."

"You always take the same route?"

"Yeh, Mister Johnston likes that four-mile drive on the back road in the morning. Says the peaceful scenery

relaxes him. There's several hundred feet of open grass
land on both sides of the road all the way down to the
river on the right and up to the foothills on the left."

"Anyone else in the limo?"

"Nope."

"No other bodyguards?"

"Naw, we weren't expecting any trouble that I knew
of."

"Go on."

"So, we were about two miles from the house when
I saw the two motorcycle cops in my side mirror. They
had their red lights flashing."

"Were you speeding?"

"Maybe a little bit, but there's never anybody to
worry about on that road so early in the morning."

"What'd you do?"

"I did what you're supposed to do, I pulled over.
How was I to know the cops were wrong."

Frankie's eyes bristled, but she kept her cool. "Keep
talking."

"One of the motorcycle cops, a tall guy, came up to
my door so I pressed the button to roll down the
window. He asked to see my driver's license. I gave it
to him like you do in a situation like that."

"What about the second person dressed like a
motorcycle policeman?"

"The second cop went around to the rear passenger
window on the other side and knocked on the glass.
Mister Johnston rolled down that window to see what
the man wanted. And that's when it all happened."

"Exactly what happened?"

"The two cops drew guns and took us prisoner. The
tall one dragged me out of the limo and tied me up to a
sign post at the side of the road."

"And Mister Johnston?"

"I couldn't see for sure with the smoked windows on the limo, but I think they tied him up in the back seat. It was him they were kidnapping for ransom, not me." The excitement of retelling the story seemed to make Jerry break out in a light film of perspiration.

Frankie sat perfectly still. "You're doing fine," she encouraged. "Now tell us about their actions when they left."

"Well," said Jerry, "the tall cop stuck a ransom note in my front pocket and told me to give it to Mister Johnston's wife. He also said to keep the law out of it and then he blindfolded me just before they drove off."

Frankie's right index finger began absently tapping on the table top. "The fake cops drove off with Mister Johnston and the limo?"

"Hey, I didn't know they weren't real cops at the time."

"How'd you get loose?"

"They didn't search me, but I had a pocket knife in my jacket, so I managed to slide my hand in the right side pocket, open the blade and cut the ropes."

"That's pretty good for one hand."

"Okay, so you got me with an illegal switchblade. All I had to do was push the button to open the blade, which was lucky for me, otherwise I could've been tied up there for hours."

Frankie nodded her acceptance. "Continue."

"I was about halfway to anywhere, but since the kidnappers told me to deliver the note, I started walking the two miles back to Mister Johnston's house."

"And you were standing on the front porch with the ransom note in your hand when our detectives drove up."

"Yeh, how'd you guys know about the kidnapping so soon?"

"Mister Johnston's wife tried to call him on his cell phone to remind him not to be late for a social engagement that evening. When she couldn't get him, she tried your cell phone."

"The kidnappers took my phone."

"You forgot to tell us about that part."

"Sorry, I didn't even think about it in all the excitement."

"We'll let that go." Then Frankie continued, "After his wife couldn't get in touch with either of you, she called the manufacturing plant, but they said you hadn't showed up, so she called the police chief who is a personal friend of the family. The chief sent a couple of detectives out to see what was going on, and there you were."

Jerry shrugged his shoulders with both palms turned outward.

"I told you everything I know."

"Let's go over the facts one more time."

"Are you saying my story doesn't add up?"

Frankie grinned for the first time. "You can put it that way if you like, or you can claim it's a matter of math."

QUESTION: What does Detective Francine Caldera find wrong with Jerry Landreth's story?

SOLUTION: Take three vehicles and four people: if one person, the bodyguard, is tied up to a road sign post; and one person, Mister Johnston, is being kidnapped; then how do two fake motorcycle cops drive off two motorcycles and a limo at the same time?

It just doesn't add up. Frankie needs to do some more investigating. Either Mister Johnston arranged his own kidnapping to get money from the company, or Jerry is one of the kidnappers and is lying about being tied up.

COME INTO MY PARLOR

There were no two ways about it, Detective Lauryn McDaniels hated spiders. Didn't make any difference if it was a miniature one crawling on the ceiling or an old web left over in an out of the way attic, they still gave her a creepy feeling. And in this decrepit mansion, which would have made a great prop for black and white Hollywood horror films half a century ago, Lauryn found herself constantly brushing aside cobwebs which hung from the rafters. She was glad to get back downstairs to the parlor and her witness waiting to be formally interviewed.

"Mister Burns," she began, "I understand you are the custodian of your uncle's family heirlooms which are worth several thousand dollars?"

"That's correct."

"And no one has been up in the attic for at least two years until this morning about an hour ago when you discovered that the lock on the staircase door had been busted?"

"That's what I told the police dispatcher when I

telephoned in the incident."

"And, you further said that when you found the broken lock, you then went upstairs to check on everything, only to discover the chest of family heirlooms normally stored at the far end of the attic had been stolen?"

"Exactly, but I have no idea who might have done such a thing."

Lauryn paused in her writing.

"How many people knew where the heirlooms were kept?"

"Only my uncle's relatives."

"Have any of those relatives been in the house lately?"

Burns stared at the ceiling for a few minutes before replying. "None that I can think of."

"But you have the only key?"

"Yes."

"And, as the caretaker of the house, you live here full time?"

"Yes."

"How difficult would it be for someone to dispose of these heirlooms?"

Burns rubbed his chin and crinkled his forehead.

"Well," he replied, "I suppose any pawn shop or history enthusiast would purchase them, or they could even be sold on E-Bay to an interested buyer."

"I see," said Lauryn. "And for the record, what did these heirlooms consist of?"

Burns went to a drawer in a nearby lamp table and withdrew a sheet of paper from a manila folder. He then returned to his over-stuffed, high-backed chair and put on his reading glasses.

"There were some private letters from the

Revolutionary War, an old tintype collection of Civil War photographs, several expensive pieces of antique jewelry set with diamonds and a few fair-sized rubies, a set of early China brought back from the Orient along with a Ming Dynasty vase, plus some other valuable odds and ends. I have a complete list here."

Lauryn took the sheet of paper.

"Thanks, I'll have a copy made for our files. We'll also check with the pawn shops, plus I'll have a criminal analyst search any internet listings for these items, but I seriously doubt we'll find anything at this time."

She studied her notes for a moment before broaching the next subject.

"I assume you have insurance to cover the theft?"

"Yes, of course. My uncle insisted that his heirlooms be insured."

Burns stood up from his chair and brushed the wrinkles out of his suit coat sleeves.

"Will there be anything else?"

Lauryn also rose to her feet.

"I understand your uncle died last night and the funeral will be on Friday. You have my condolences."

"Thank you," replied Burns. "I hope you catch the thieves. Stealing from a dead man is a despicable thing to do."

"I quite agree with you," said Detective Lauryn McDaniels as she thoughtfully tapped her notebook with the end of her ball point pen. "But then I don't think we will have very far to look."

QUESTION: Why did Detective McDaniels believe she wouldn't have far to look?

SOLUTION: If Burns had traipsed to the far end of

21

the attic and back again an hour earlier as he claimed, then Detective Lauryn McDaniels should not have been brushing off all the spider webs she found when she went up to view the alleged scene of the crime. More than likely, Burns sold off the heirlooms as he needed money and then panicked after his uncle died and knew that relatives would be inquiring about the valuable heirlooms.

GRAVE TROUBLE

Sheriff Angie Kliewer didn't appreciate getting called out of a comfortable bed before it was time to get up. Yet when the telephone rang this early in the morning, it somehow always ended up that her only night shift deputy happened to be working on the other side of the county, or was otherwise deeply occupied, whenever a disaster managed to occur outside of regular office hours. She dressed quickly, told her husband he still had forty-five minutes before the alarm went off, then buckled on her gun belt and headed for the coffee pot.

Half an hour later, Angie pulled into the gravel driveway of a prominent businessman who'd had a troubled past. She parked beside the horse stable behind the house, grabbed her cup of half-brewed coffee from the console and began walking toward all the commotion going on out in the pasture. In the knee-high grass, several men stood gathered around a backhoe at the far end of a trench. They seemed to be staring down into the dirt. Angie sized up the situation and decided to start her investigation with the backhoe operator, especially since he'd been the one who called in the problem.

"Harvey, what's going on here?"

"Well, Sheriff, the man who owns this place hired me to dig this four-foot deep trench so he could drain that soggy ground they've got up there." Harvey gestured over his shoulder. "After explaining to me what all he wanted, the owner left yesterday about noon for a few days of fun in Las Vegas. Me, I worked all afternoon, quitting about dusk. Then when I came back early this morning to start again, I noticed part of a leather shoe sticking out of the loose dirt down there at the bottom. I got down in the ditch with a shovel and that's when I found out somebody was still wearing that shoe, so I called your dispatcher right away."

"Did you move or touch anything?"

"Well, I used the shovel to dig loose dirt from the shoe and up toward this end of the trench, but only got as far as the guy's belt. After that, I didn't want to go any farther."

"That's fine, Harvey. The crime scene investigators will be here pretty soon. They can finish the digging."

Angie jumped over the narrow trench to view the ditch from the other side.

"Tell me something, Harvey. You've been doing excavating work in this county for several years. What's that horizontal black line there in the dirt wall about three inches down from the top?"

Harvey dropped down on one knee.

"I see that stuff a lot, Sheriff. This land used to be all thick forest until about fifty years ago when a fire went through. Burnt everything down to the ground. Even sterilized the soil for a couple of years until heavy rains caused landslides of mud to come down from the higher ground. After that the grass grew in. Now it's all pasture land."

"And that thicker white line about ten inches down from the top?"

"That's a thin layer of limestone, it runs through all the hills in these parts."

About then, Angie heard a van door slam shut behind her, and glanced up to recognize the state boys with their mobile crime lab. She motioned to the newcomers.

"Over here."

After several measurements and photographs, the evidence technicians finally uncovered the rest of the body. The senior tech bent over, extracted a billfold from the victim's back pocket and pulled out a driver's license.

"Anybody you know?"

Angie glanced over the tech's shoulder at the name and license photo.

"We got a missing persons circular on that guy a couple of days ago," she said in a low voice.

"Well now you've found him."

"How long has he been deceased?"

"Best guess? Preliminary tests show about forty-eight hours. We'll be able to tell you more later."

"Anything you can give me now?"

"Yeah. He's a middle-aged male, he's dead and it looks like a gunshot did it. The rest will have to wait for forensics."

"I think you missed something big here."

"What's that?"

"Harvey's backhoe didn't dig him up."

The senior tech stopped writing in his notebook and

stared down into the four-foot deep trench.

"The victim's laying right there at the bottom of the ditch. What do you mean the backhoe didn't dig him up?"

Angie gave a grim smile.

"I think the killer is trying to implicate the owner of this land. We need to look for someone with a grudge against both the victim and the land owner."

"Why's that?"

"The victim was obviously planted here after the trench was started."

QUESTION: Why did Sheriff Angie Kliewer think the body had been "planted" after the trench work started?

SOLUTION: If the body had been buried in the pasture earlier, then the ground would have been disturbed, in which case the black line of carbon from the burnt forest and the white line of limestone found on both walls of the trench would have been broken and mixed into the soil when the grave was filled back in. But since these two lines were unbroken, it is more likely that the killer waited until nightfall after the ditch work had been partially completed. He then planted the victim in the bottom of the trench and covered the body with loose dirt so it could be found the next morning, thus casting immediate suspicion on a third party, the owner of the land.

KEEPING UP WITH INSPECTOR JONES

"I 've got all the suspects lined up in the den," Corporal Davis reported. "Anyway, I think it's the den, but with this house being under new construction, I'm not really sure. There's nothing but bare 2x4's, plywood walls and a cement foundation. At this point, most of the rooms look similar to me."

Inspector Jones merely nodded. He was more interested in studying the white chalk line which had previously been drawn around the body on the bare wood floor, before the coroner had taken the victim away.

"Forensics done yet?"

"They're packing up to leave."

"Good. Tell me about our victim."

Corporal Davis took out his notebook and flipped open the cover. "Mister Conrad was the developer for this new, high-end, gated community and this lot is where the first house is being built." Then looking up from his notebook, he added, "It appears to be a nice place out here in the woods. Too bad someone killed him."

"What did the security guard at the gate have to say?"

"The guard said four other people were already here this morning when Mister Conrad arrived. By the way, I checked the surveillance camera at the gate and it shows the guard never left his post, so we can remove him from the list."

"Very good," replied the Inspector, "then that leaves us with only four suspects. Tell me about them."

"There's a carpenter, a plumber, a painter and an electrician. They were the only ones inside the house with the victim."

"Who found the body?" inquired the Inspector.

Corporal Davis flipped a couple of pages. "About fifteen minutes after the developer arrived, the electrician said he came in from the Master Bedroom to run wire up to where a couple of wall sockets would be placed. He claims the victim was already lying on the floor when he went into the room. He then used his cell phone to call the guard who in turn notified the police. I was the first responder and secured the scene until more uniforms arrived."

"What about the other three contractors?"

"The plumber claimed he was down in the basement, stubbing in some pipe. The painter said he was taking a break in the kitchen and drinking coffee out of his thermos. The carpenter was allegedly upstairs measuring out where the second story walls would be built. All four of them claimed to be so engrossed in their activities that they didn't hear anything unusual that morning, but then the carpenter did have a loud radio playing."

Inspector Jones looked up from his observation of the chalk line. "Can any of these contractors vouch for the others' whereabouts?"

"No sir, they all say they had their own jobs to do and don't remember seeing any of the others after Mister Conrad showed up to check on progress."

"I see," said the Inspector as he removed a small digital recorder from his jacket pocket. "Well, it's time to start the interviewing process. This room will be as good a place as any, where the chalk lines make a good backdrop to encourage a confession from the guilty one."

The Corporal nodded his agreement. "Which contractor would you like me to bring in first?"

"Why," replied the Inspector, "the one that doesn't belong here."

QUESTION: Which contractor does the Inspector suspect of not having a good reason to be inside this first house under construction in the new development? And why doesn't this contractor belong here?

SOLUTION: The carpenter should be here because he's building the walls, floors and roof out of 2x4's, plywood and rafters. The plumber has to be in this house under construction because he needs to run PVC pipes through the framework before the walls can be enclosed with wallboard. And, the electrician also needs to be in the uncompleted house in order to run wiring to all parts of the house before the walls are enclosed. But why is the painter here? He has absolutely nothing to paint at this stage of the house building. He may not be the guilty party, but he does have a lot of explaining to do for his presence at a murder scene.

IN PLAIN VIEW

Homicide Detective Oscar plopped down in the front passenger side of the squad car and turned to Corporal Davis sitting in the driver's seat.

"What have you got?"

"I was right around the corner," replied Corporal Davis, "when a radio call reported a violent disturbance and a body at that ground floor apartment across the street." He used his thumb to indicate a three-story brick building on the opposite side of the street.

Detective Oscar noted the street address.

"When I arrived on scene," continued Corporal Davis, "there was a man standing on the sidewalk. He claimed to have seen everything while looking through the front picture window."

"So, we have an eye-witness?" inquired Oscar.

"Yes sir." Davis then pointed to a man seated in the back of the squad car. "His name is Jerry Slack."

Detective Oscar rotated far enough in the front seat to face their eye-witness.

"Mister Slack, tell me what you saw."

"Well," said the man in the back seat, "I was walking up the sidewalk when I happened to glance across the street at that apartment over there at ground level. The light was kind of dim inside, but I could plainly see two men fighting in what looked to be a living room. One of the men had a golf club in his hand and struck the other guy, who then fell to the floor."

Detective Oscar jotted down some notes.

"What did you do then?"

"I didn't know what to do. Guess I was still standing here when your uniformed officer pulled up, but I can describe the guy with the club."

Detective Oscar wrote down a detailed description of the alleged attacker.

"He must've gone out the back door of the building," added Mr. Slack, "because I didn't see him come out this way."

Oscar thanked the eye-witness, and then turned his attention back to Corporal Davis.

"Have you checked out the apartment?"

"Nope, just got here a couple of minutes before you and was finding out about the situation from our witness. Nobody else has responded yet, and as you know, we're running a little short-handed on man power today."

"Okay," replied Oscar, "you stay with our witness and I'll take a look inside the apartment."

Getting out of the squad car, Detective Oscar drew his service weapon, crossed the street and entered the building. He found the front door to the ground floor apartment open wide. Cautiously, he stepped inside.

Yep, there was a body on the floor and a golf club was lying close by. The eye-witness was right about that part.

In hopes of providing more light inside the room, Detective Oscar used his elbow to click a nearby wall switch into the up position. Nothing happened, the bulb must have been burned out. Being careful where he put his feet, Oscar stepped over to the wall and pulled a cord to open the front drapes so daylight could add some brightness to the crime scene.

Using all the techniques they'd taught him at the police academy, Oscar then moved through the rest of the rooms to ensure there was no one else in the apartment. He couldn't help thinking that the witness was correct about the dim lighting inside, however, there was one very obvious fact that bothered him about the entire situation. In his opinion, their eye-witness was lying and should probably be in handcuffs.

QUESTION: Why does Detective Oscar think Mr. Slack is lying, what is he lying about and why should he be in handcuffs?

SOLUTION: The eye-witness claims he saw the violent incident through the picture window in the living room while he was across the street. However, after Detective Oscar entered the apartment and wanted better lighting to see by, but the wall switch didn't work, he opened the living room drapes to let in sun light. If the drapes had been in a closed position, then no alleged eye-witness from across the street could have seen anyone with a golf club strike another person. Yet because Mr. Slack knew details of an event he couldn't see from outside, that meant he must have been inside the apartment during the incident.

ONE FOR THE ROAD

J essie Walker opened the insulated door to the large walk-in and observed the contents of the normally refrigerated room. Sagging cardboard boxes were stacked from the floor to the ceiling.

"You might not want to breathe too deep," Mr. Cutter said. "The storm took out our electricity for a couple of days, and as you can plainly see, Ms. Walker, we lost all the produce in our warehouse."

From the doorway, Jessie carefully counted the boxes of lettuce and jotted that number down on her insurance claim form. Finished, she stepped aside to let Mr. Cutter close the door.

"Now that you've seen the last of our damaged goods, we can go to my office and fill out your paperwork in comfort."

Stepping inside the office door first, Cutter flipped on the light switch. Overhead florescent tubes snapped into life.

"When did your power come back on?" Jessie asked. She quickly installed herself in a chair on the visitor's side of his desk in order to have a stable writing surface.

"Shortly before you got here. I'd say less than an hour ago."

"Did the entire city black out?"

"No, just parts of it. Guess we were in the unlucky part of town. The electric company is still making repairs."

"Does your company have an emergency generator to supply electricity during a power outage?" she inquired. "Most companies dealing in refrigerated products have a backup generator for circumstances like these."

Mr. Cutter got a sheepish look on his face.

"As a matter of fact, we do have one. However, we couldn't get it started. It's an older model and I probably should've replaced it before this, but the truth is we're a small operation on a shoe string budget and couldn't afford the extra expense at this time."

"Business been a little slow?"

"You can say that. Big produce suppliers work on a larger margin than we do, so they undercut our prices. Our small company's cash flow can be a problem sometimes, yet we still have to pay our bills."

"How many employees do you have?" asked Jessie.

"We've got two truck drivers, both of which were out making deliveries when the power went down. The secretary went home long before the storm hit, but she doesn't know how to start up the generator anyhow. A couple of local high school kids usually come in for a part time work shift in the afternoons if we have any semis to unload, but there haven't been any loads for the last few days. And then there's me. I do the buying and oversee the entire operation."

"Where were you when the power went out?"

"On the interstate, the other side of town. I took shelter under an overpass for several hours. By the time I got here, the produce lockers had already lost most of any refrigeration they had."

Jessie filled in two more blocks on the insurance claim form. "I suppose it would have been cost prohibitive to cover the vegetables with ice?"

"We'd have needed a couple of trucks full of ice to cover all our produce. By the time I got here after the storm blew over and found out the extent of the problem, every place in town was already sold out of ice, as far as large quantities go anyway. Guess everybody was trying to save the food in their freezers at home."

Jessie took out a pocket calculator and placed it on the desk. "I'll add up the figures you gave me on the damaged goods and see what we're looking at for a claim."

"Sure," replied Mr. Cutter. "Tell you what, it's been two long stressful days around here, so I'm going to have a mixed drink to settle my nerves. One for the road you might say, since I'll be chalking up a lot of windshield time later this week to start the supply process going all over again. Can I get you anything?"

"Just some bottled water would be fine, thank you. I've got a long drive myself back to the home office."

Cutter swiveled his executive office chair around in order to open a door in the credenza behind him. He removed a half full bottle of bourbon and a water tumbler. Setting both these items on his desk, he then walked over to the mini refrigerator along the side wall. He returned with two bottles of spring water and a plastic tray of ice cubes. One bottle was placed in front of Jessie. He then twisted the plastic tray until several ice cubes fell into the water tumbler. Bourbon was added and the second water bottle opened to fill up the remainder of the glass tumbler.

"Here's to better days," he said.

Jessie just looked at him.

QUESTION: Jessie saw the damaged produce with her own eyes, but what made her think she needed to take a closer look at Mr. Cutter's receipts and documents before processing his insurance claim?

SOLUTION: The storm had knocked out power to parts of the city, and according to Mr. Cutter, his produce company was in one of those unlucky parts of town. If his electricity had been down for two days with no working generator to supply backup electricity, then how did his mini refrigerator make ice cubes in less than hour for his mixed drink? It's very possible that Cutter let his overstocked produce go bad in order to receive an insurance check to help out his small company's cash flow, or else he may have brought in another company's ruined produce to place in his refrigeration lockers so he could file a fraudulent claim for his own benefit.

OFFICER IT WAS SELF DEFENSE

Harry slipped a pair of cloth booties onto his street shoes as he stepped into the front doorway of the house. That was one thing about being on the Homicide Squad all these years; Forensics was always coming up with newer procedures in order to keep the crime scene from becoming contaminated. Now, everybody entering one of these yellow taped off areas had to wear the darn things over their shoes.

"Down the hall, first room on the left," said the uniform at the front door after seeing Harry's gold shield dangling from a chain around his neck.

Taking his time getting there, Harry paused occasionally to notice several paintings along the wall. From the little bit he knew about art, these seemed old and possibly very valuable.

In the study, he found two members of the Forensic Team; one operating a video camera, while the other member set up a machine for measuring distances to various objects in the room. More procedures and newfangled gadgets as far as Harry was concerned. Whatever happened to old fashioned detecting, he wondered.

Stopping a few feet away, he got his first look at the body lying on the floor. It was a well-dressed younger man, on his back, with two bullet holes in his chest. Bright light from the Forensic Team's video camera glittered in the small shards of glass on the chest and shoulders of the victim's expensive suit coat. To the victim's right side, a large smooth rock rested on a red and gold Persian carpet. Harry figured the rock came from a decorative garden he could see just outside the damaged French doors about three feet beyond the man's head. One of the two French doors had a huge hole in the glass as if something had been thrown through it. To the victim's left lay two shiny brass casings from an automatic pistol. Both casings had plastic markers nearby to denote their evidence numbers in this case.

"Looks pretty simple to me," said Harry.

"Glad to hear you say that," his Captain growled, walking up behind him. "Forensics and a couple of your fellow detectives have been doing all the work while we were waiting for you to get here."

Harry ignored the implication of him arriving late. "What kind of story did you get on this?" he inquired to change the subject.

"Homeowner's an art dealer," replied the Captain, "a somewhat older gentleman than the victim. Said he was here alone doing some paperwork when the doorbell rang. He looked through the peephole in the door and saw a man he'd been having trouble with over a painting. Told the dissatisfied customer to come to his gallery on Monday morning and they'd talk there. The man walked away. Next thing the homeowner knew, there were loud noises outside the study, so he got his pistol and went to investigate."

"What'd he find," asked Harry.

"He said the disgruntled customer threw a rock through the glass of one of the French doors, reached through the hole, unlocked the doors and stormed in, so he shot the guy twice before any harm could come to himself. Claims self-defense on his part. Want to talk with him?"

Harry nodded. "Yeah, but I think we'd better do it down at the station where we can tape his interview."

QUESTION: Why does Harry want to treat the homeowner as a suspect in this case rather than seeing the situation as a matter of self-defense?

SOLUTION: Harry noticed small shards of glass on the chest and shoulders of the victim's suit. If the victim had thrown the rock as claimed, then the glass should have gone inside the study while the man was still outside. Harry suspects the homeowner let the man inside, they argued in the study and the homeowner shot him. Then, to concoct an alibi, the homeowner went outside and threw the rock through his own French door to make the scene appear to be a break in. As the rock came through the glass, shards travelled inward and landed on the victim's suit as he lay already dead on the Persian carpet.

"ONE STEP AT A TIME"

Mattie had an instant dislike for the only known witness to the crime. In her mind, Paul Sanders seemed too smug, too sure of himself. But, as a homicide detective, Mattie knew she had to operate on more than just personal feelings. If she could find a discrepancy in his story, then maybe there would be something to work with. She'd start with the basics and take it one step at a time.

"When did all this happen?"

Sanders turned his wheelchair toward the clock on the wall before answering.

"About an hour ago. I'd say it was close to seven PM when I called the police, which was right after I heard the shots upstairs...and then Albert didn't come back down."

"You're referring to Albert Petersen, your business partner?"

"Correct. He came over to ask some questions about our company cash flow. Appears there were some transactions he had trouble following in the books, but

40

then Petersen's never been very good with figures."

"Go on."

"To pacify him, I sent him upstairs to find some of my personal business papers from last year. I had stored them in the safe in my old bedroom, long before the car accident which put me in this chair. In any case, I gave Petersen the combination and told him to go on up and retrieve the necessary paperwork. For some reason, he believed those documents might shed light on financial problems our company has been having lately."

"Excuse me," Mattie interrupted. "You made mention of your old bedroom?"

"Yes, after my accident several months ago, I could no longer climb the stairs and there is no elevator in the house. The doctors say I may never walk again, so I had a bed set up in the main floor study. That's now my new bedroom. As you can see, I'm pretty much confined to living on the main floor."

Mattie started jotting down some quick notes, asking her next question while writing at the same time.

"So, your partner, Mister Petersen, came over this evening, you talked for a while about company business, he went upstairs for some paperwork and then you heard the shots. How many shots?"

"Three, there were exactly three."

"Who else was in the house?"

"No one."

Mattie kept writing.

"Do you employ a housekeeper?"

"Well yes, I do have a lady in twice a week to do the cleaning and laundry."

"Was this one of her days to work here?"

"Yes, but she leaves about five o'clock in the afternoon, therefore my cleaning lady was already gone before Petersen arrived."

"Therefore, it was just you and Mister Petersen in the house at the time?"

"Correct, except of course for the burglar who was evidently upstairs."

"The burglar?"

"Yes, the one who shot Petersen."

Mattie paused in her writing.

"How do you know it was a burglar?"

"The first patrolman to arrive went upstairs to see what happened. When he came back down, he said the sliding glass door that leads out onto the bedroom balcony had been jimmied open from the outside. Some of my personal belongings had been strewn around the room, plus jewelry and cash were missing from the safe. Obviously, it had to be the work of a burglar. Anyone with half a brain can see that for themselves. Petersen must have surprised the man and been shot for his efforts."

"But you never heard any noises upstairs before the shots?"

"No, the burglar must have been fairly experienced in being quiet, but then he probably expected that in my current condition I wouldn't be coming upstairs anyway. For Petersen to go up was merely a fluke. Call it bad luck or poor timing."

Mattie took this time to record notes on Sanders's appearance from the top down.

Well styled hair. His suit looked very expensive and she recognized his tie as imported silk. His finger nails were manicured. The man obviously had money and an ego for self-image. No apparent bloodstains on his clothing, and there were no spots which looked like recent attempts at cleaning them. The shoes appeared to be almost new, with a slight crease across the top, but well shined. Probably Italian leather. No bloodstains there either.

"Would you mind rolling forward a few feet so I can inspect the wheels on your chair?"

"Not at all, detective."

Sanders did as requested. "Satisfied?"

Nothing seemed visible on the wheels or frame of the chair, but she had to check. Mattie laid down her notepad and pen, then rubbed her forehead in thought for a minute.

"Not quite," she replied. "When the forensic people get finished upstairs, I want them to swab your hands for gun powder residue."

"Me," exclaimed Sanders, "but I'm in a wheelchair. I couldn't have gone upstairs to shoot Petersen, and if I had shot him downstairs, then how did his body get upstairs?"

Mattie slowly shook her head.

"There's a problem with your story, Mister Sanders. I think you left a step out."

QUESTION: Why did Homicide Detective Mattie want to have the forensics people swab Sanders' hands for gun powder?

SOLUTION: A person in a wheelchair should not have creases across the top of their fairly new shoes. Creases in shoe leather across the top occur when the foot bends forward to take a step. Therefore, Detective Mattie has suspicion to believe that Sanders can actually walk, regardless of what he says about his physical condition after the car accident.

THE ALMOST CLEVER THIEF

Vice Detective Oscar, on loan to the overworked Burglary Squad, detested cold, rainy weather such as the city had been receiving for the last twenty-four hours. All this excess humidity made the hairs of his long mustache droop and gave his face the appearance of a drenched cat. He expected to take a lot of kidding when he got back to the station, but there was nothing he could do about it for now.

Resigned to circumstances, he stuck both hands deep in the pockets of his trench coat and peered at the tool marks on the back door of the jewelry store. The door hung by one hinge on the right side. Yep, somebody had definitely pried it open to gain entry. And, they must have had a drawing of the store's layout because they'd been in, opened the safe and gotten out in a short time without anyone knowing they were here. The call had only come in about an hour ago. His suspicions were quickly confirmed when another detective handed him a piece of paper.

"The owner's nephew said he found this note lying in the alley this morning after he opened the store and noticed their burgled safe. Says the note was just outside the jimmied back door. Looks like maybe the burglars dropped it in their hurry to leave."

Oscar removed his gloved hands from his trench coat pockets and took the note. Carefully, he smoothed the crisp white paper against his police notebook and studied the paper's contents. At the top was a list of three names with question marks after each name. At the bottom was a rough drawing of the store's interior.

"All three of those names are expert safe crackers," said the other detective. "Anyone of them could have done this job."

Oscar considered the background of each man on the list.

According to police intel, Ihor Stravinski had an impressive record of big scores, four arrests, but no convictions. He was a golden boy, allegedly trained by an old time safe cracker and sometimes used by the local Russian mafia on special jobs, at least that was the word on the streets. He was a left hander as Oscar recalled. One of these days, Ihor would slip up and get caught. Was this the day?

Then there was Hector Carrillo, an import from the other coast who had loose ties to several criminal organizations. Hector had been down twice, but seemed to be getting smarter in his old age. There'd been a recent newspaper article about Hector being hauled in for questioning concerning a similar job on the north side, but the police had to let him go for lack of evidence. Hector would be one to definitely keep in mind.

And, of course there was Tommy Jones, a local

home-grown boy who'd once had a promising career with an out of town safe company where he'd learned all the inner workings before his supervisors caught him trying to open their own office safe. He'd returned to his home town and now seemed to have lots of spending money even though he was currently unemployed. Tommy would be a good one to keep an eye on in the future. Oscar made himself a mental note to see if the jewelry store safe and the safe company that had previously employed Tommy were the same brand. Over the years, Oscar had learned not to believe in coincidence when it came to crime.

"So, what do you think?" inquired the other detective. "Who's your prime suspect for this job?"

After a moment's reflection, Oscar gave a smile barely visible under his bedraggled mustache.

"This particular thief was almost clever, but he made at least one mistake."

QUESTION: Who does Oscar suspect and why?

SOLUTION: It's been raining for the last twenty-four hours, yet the note that the owner's nephew allegedly found lying out in the alley by the jimmied back door is still crisp when Oscar smooths out the paper against his police notebook. The note with the names and interior drawing of the store was obviously planted by the nephew otherwise it would be soggy and limp, much like Oscar's mustache.

ONE WRONG STEP

My cell phone rang a little after midnight. Actually, it was more of a chirping sound, but most people still prefer to say their phone is ringing, so I go with that. I kept one hand on the steering wheel, removed the phone from my handbag with the other, opened the phone and placed the receiver next to my ear. Caller ID on the screen had already told me it was Alexis on the other end. She wasn't my best friend, but I had to admit we seemed to be on good speaking terms lately.

"Hello."

"Kari, where are you?"

"I was out to a charity reception. I'm almost home now."

"Have you talked to Moira lately?"

"Not for a few days. Why?"

"I can't get her to answer her phone and no one seems to have seen her for the last day or two."

"Maybe she went on a trip somewhere."

"If she did, she didn't tell me. Look, I'm driving out

to her house right now, why don't you meet me there?"

I reflected on how Alexis and Moira had recently competed for the attention of the same handsome widower who'd been in play for the last several years, a man who was the almost wealthy owner of a local company. Moira had won out in the end and their wedding was set for next June. I wasn't sure what interest Alexis still had in Moira, but that's when my curiosity kicked in. And you know what they say about curiosity and the cat.

"Okay, Alexis, I'll be there in about ten minutes."

"Good, I'll wait for you at the front door if I get there first."

Several minutes later, I pulled into the driveway and cut the engine. From where I sat, the house was dark, no lights in any of the rooms I could see from the front. Less than thirty seconds later, Alexis pulled her car in right behind me. I got out and lingered by my vehicle until she approached. She gave a little wave. I nodded. Without exchanging further hellos, we walked up to the house together. I rang the front doorbell. No answer. I tried the door. Locked.

"She usually keeps a key under the flower pot," remarked Alexis.

To prove her point, she tilted the flower pot resting on the porch near the front door and extracted a shiny metal object from beneath the pottery. She held the silver colored key out in her right hand. I took the key, unlocked the heavy wood door and pushed it open.

"Moira," I called out.

No answer. The interior of the house appeared tomb dark, and neither of us had a flashlight. I searched for the wall switch with my free hand and turned on the overhead foyer lights. The hallway leading to the rear of the house seemed eerie and deserted.

"We better stay together," Alexis whispered.

Room by room, we turned on floor lamps and overhead lights to take a look around. Nothing seemed out of place. Gradually, all that was left for us to search on the main floor was the study at the rear of the house. After that we'd have to climb the stairs and check any rooms on the second floor. I reached inside the doorway of the downstairs study and flailed for a wall switch.

"No overhead light in here," said Alexis, "only a lamp on a mahogany end table at the far side of the room. The lamp's got one of those three-way bulbs in it. Wait here and I'll turn it on."

She walked into the silent darkness.

I didn't hear a sound other than the scraping of her shoes on the carpet until the lamp clicked on. Then she turned toward me and gasped. On the floor between us lay a body stretched out perpendicular to the burgundy leather couch positioned along the wall. On the far side of the burgundy couch was the end table which Alexis had mentioned and the now glowing lamp that threw light into the room.

"Oh my," gasped Alexis, "it's Moira. Someone's killed her."

At first glance, I had to admit Moira didn't look too good, especially with a bullet wound in her chest. I checked for a pulse at her throat, but her heart rate was zero. Quickly, I looked around at the floor and couch. With no gun to be found in the vicinity, it obviously wasn't a case of suicide. Alexis appeared to be right, someone had killed Moira.

"We better call the police," Alexis said in a low voice, "and let them handle it."

I quickly agreed and stepped out of the room. Removing my cell phone from my handbag, I punched in 9-1-1. The answering voice was welcome to my ear.

"Police emergency. How may I help you?"

"There's been a murder," I exclaimed. Then I whispered into the phone. "And if you hurry, I think you'll find your suspect still here."

QUESTION: What mistake did Alexis make in order to become a suspect?

SOLUTION: Alexis' shoes scraped on the carpet as she walked into the dark study. For Alexis to walk across the dark room without stumbling into the body and making an outcry before the lights came on, she had to know where the body already was and therefore stepped over it in order to reach the end table at the far end of the room and then turn on the lamp. By telephoning me to meet her, Alexis was merely trying to have the body found, plus as a witness to the crime scene, it potentially allowed her some access to the police investigation soon to be conducted.

THE CASE HINGED ON

In search of a birthday gift, Rita pushed open the front glass door leading into a small jewelry store just in time to hear a gunshot fired in the backroom. The only noise to be heard in the sudden following silence was the fading away sound of the electric bell which went off every time the front door was opened or closed. Now with one foot inside the store and the other still out on the sidewalk, Rita held the door ajar with one hand, in case she had to make a hasty retreat.

"Hello?" she called.

After a moment's hesitation, there was a thud, then a scuffling of shoe leather and a man's voice shouted from the backroom. "Quick, we have to call the police. The manager's been shot."

A stocky man with graying hair, and wearing a charcoal grey pinstripe suit rushed out of the backroom, snatched up the receiver from a wall phone behind the jewelry counter and began punching in numbers.

Rita stepped farther into the store. The door swung

shut behind her.

"What happened?"

"We were robbed," gasped the man. Then he began speaking into the phone and Rita listened carefully as the grey-haired store employee related all the details to the police operator on the other end of the line. "About ten minutes ago. A robber held us at gunpoint in the backroom. He made our manager open the safe. Then he stuck all the jewels in a bag and headed for the back door. There had to be several thousands of dollars worth of diamonds in that bag not to mention the other jewelry he took. When our manager started after him, the robber fired one shot and the manager collapsed on the floor. No, no pulse. I'm pretty sure he's dead."

As she listened to more of the conversation, Rita advanced all the way up to the jewelry counter where the employee stood on the other side. To her ears, his voice definitely sounded strained.

"Describe the robber? Sure. About five foot ten, medium build, brown hair, a scar on his right cheek, had black leather driving gloves on his hands and should be easy to spot because he was wearing a red windbreaker and a black ball cap. Oh yeah, the name embroidered in white on the upper left front of his windbreaker was 'George'."

The employee paused for breath.

"Armed? I don't think he is now. He dropped the gun in front of the back door after he shot our manager. Then the robber went out the back door and slammed it shut behind him. Once he got in the alley, he could've gone anywhere. No, I didn't see a car."

Being the curious type she was, Rita leaned slightly over the jewelry counter to see into the backroom for herself. The room was well lighted. And yes, the body of a well-dressed man was lying in the middle of the floor. His back was to Rita, so she couldn't see his face or any bullet wounds, but in any case, she figured this had to be the manager.

"Right," said the store employee into the phone, "I won't touch anything and I'll wait here until the police arrive."

Rita stood on tiptoes to see farther into the backroom. By craning her neck a little to the right, she caught the shininess of three silver colored door hinges and a slightly tarnished doorknob. This had to be the back door that the robber went out. Rita observed the bottom of the black metal door. There on the floor up against the metal lay a large revolver. This had to be the murder weapon. Everything that the employee had mentioned to the police seemed to be right there in plain sight.

The grey-haired employee hung up the phone.

Rita came off her tiptoes and stepped back from the counter.

"It's a good thing you came in and set off the electric bell when you did," said the employee, "otherwise the robber might have shot me too. I think you scared him off just in time."

Rita smiled politely.

After that, there was nothing to do until the police came screeching up in the first two patrol cars. A burly sergeant quickly took command of the crime scene and sent one patrolman around into the alley to cover the back door while another patrolman secured the front. Yellow crime scene tape sprung up outside the store like magic neon ribbons.

Behind the counter, the sergeant immediately cornered the grey-haired employee and started scribbling notes into a small spiral notebook.

Since none of the patrolmen had said anything to her, Rita wasn't sure what she was supposed to do, so she waited patiently until the first unmarked police car drove up and parked in the street.

Two men in rumpled suits got out of the car, passed through the yellow crime scene tape and opened the front door. The electric bell chimed. Both men approached the sergeant.

"What have we got?" inquired the younger of the two plain clothes detectives.

Rita decided now was the time. She tugged on the suit coat sleeve of the older detective until he looked in her direction.

"I think I can tell you the killer's mistake," she whispered. "The case all hinges on..."

QUESTION: What evidence makes Rita think she can show who the killer is and the mistake he made?

SOLUTION: Since Rita could see the three door hinges on the inside of the exit door, that meant the door to the alley opened into the backroom, not outward. And if the robber/killer had dropped the gun in front of the back door after firing the deadly shot and then left by that same door, as the grey-haired employee claimed, the gun could not possibly have been lying up against the door. Yet as Rita plainly observed, the revolver was positioned against the back door...where the employee had thrown it.

THE DEVIL'S IN THE DETAILS

Kaitlyn had remained under cover at the edge of the tree line since sunup this morning. Now came late afternoon with long shadows stretching up across the sloping grass meadow to her front. Through binoculars, she'd observed the old castle on the other side of the meadow for several hours. Only one car had driven up the gravel road from the valley below, and other than a brief glimpse of the vehicle's driver, she had seen no one else. She started mapping out a plan to enter the castle without being seen.

Yesterday, she'd been sipping coffee at a sidewalk café in Rome when her employer slid back a chair and joined her at the small table.

"We have a rush job for you."

"Haste makes mistakes," she replied.

"We just got the information." He paused. "And you're the best qualified to do this."

Kaitlyn reflected on his statement. True, she had acquired several questionable skills in her shadowed past, skills her employer needed for the type of work they did. But then she was only authorized to use these talents in foreign countries where her employer had a mandate.

Over the years, her reputation for the successful completion of dangerous jobs had grown. Thankfully, only her employer knew her true identity. The opposition had never obtained so much as a fleeting glimpse of her face; they only saw the residue of her handiwork. To them, she remained a ghost in the night. With luck on her part it would stay that way.

Being constantly abroad for long periods of time, she soon became fluent in several languages. Plus, the deep immersion in foreign cultures made her keenly aware of the small distinct differences to be observed in any community. This awareness of the little things in life kept her senses sharp, kept her alive.

Kaitlyn studied her employer's face.

"What's the job?"

"Photograph the contents of a locked briefcase."

"Who's your source?"

"An intelligence officer for the East Germans, or was before the wall came down. Now he's fallen on hard times, needs money."

"Why the rush?"

"We got a ten hour window."

"Go on."

Her employer discretely checked to ensure no one could overhear their conversation before he continued.

"There's a castle in the mountains. It was once the keep of a feudal lord who extracted tolls from pilgrims traveling through the passes of northern Italy toward the Holy Land. Now the castle serves as a safe house for a terrorist organization. Their courier arrives at the castle tomorrow night and departs the next morning.

That's our window."

From the folds of a newspaper, her employer laid out aerial photographs. They showed the castle with a sheer drop on the north and east sides, a steep incline below the south wall and a grassy meadow in front of the main gate in the west wall. Kaitlyn quickly determined the only acceptable approach was along the west wall.

"Security?"

"According to our informant, a motion activated camera is mounted on the outside wall above the main gate. Despite the camera, he claims a top agent could find a way in. No dogs on the premises and only one armed guard is known to patrol the inside grounds."

Kaitlyn had then accepted the challenge. Now, from her vantage point in the trees, she watched a flock of sheep slowly graze their way down from the ridgeline on her left. They passed through the tall grass meadow between her and the castle and soon disappeared.

As evening shadows deepened across the empty meadow, Kaitlyn changed into her black ops gear. Dark clothes, climbing shoes, ropes, spy camera, penlight, lock picks, .22 caliber pistol with silencer, all new and untraceable equipment.

For several minutes, she contemplated the area she had to cross. No visible activity in the meadow, or along the castle walls. Turning her wrist, she glanced at her black faced Rolex. Almost time. If all went as planned, she would return to this same hiding spot, pick up any equipment left behind, hike down the hill to her car concealed in a grove of birch near the main highway, and drive south to a small farmhouse where her employer waited for the information from the courier's pouch.

When the castle walls were still well silhouetted

against the horizon, Kaitlyn left the tree line and snake crawled across the meadow. Fifteen minutes of keeping low brought her to the edge of the gravel road which came down from the castle's main gate, ran parallel near the castle wall and descended into the valley below. Barely raising her head above the tall grass cover, she looked north to see if the security camera above the main gate had detected her trip across the meadow. No, the camera still pointed up along the ridgeline. Her movements hadn't been seen, and she was now safely out of peripheral range of the camera's motion sensors.

Taking one more cautionary glance in both directions, Kaitlyn dashed across the road and flattened herself against the castle wall. She listened carefully. No suspicious noise came to her ears. After rubbing rosin on her fingertips for traction, she started up the stone wall. Ten feet up, she froze in place. Something wasn't right. One small item was out of place. This had to be a trap.

QUESTION: What made Kaitlyn think the opposition was waiting for her?

SOLUTION: When the flock of sheep grazed their way down the slope and through the meadow between Kaitlyn and the castle, the motion detection security camera should have turned to follow the sheep downhill and then stayed in that position until its sensors caught other movement. Instead the camera remained pointed up in the direction of the ridge line. Obviously, the camera is not functioning as intended. By making a surreptitious entry easy for Kaitlyn, the opposition hoped to lure her into their grasp.

Perhaps Kaitlyn's employer needs to have another

talk with the informant who supplied the information about the castle's security.

THE MAGIC RIDE

Once again Rita found herself arriving late for the monthly businesswomen's meeting at the hotel. Quietly, so as to not call attention to her tardiness, Rita eased into the last row of chairs at the conference suite and took a seat directly behind two women she knew only by name and occupation. Both ladies, dressed in professional attire, seemed to be more interested in their personal conversation than in the speaker up front. And it wasn't that Rita was eavesdropping, but the two women were talking just loud enough that she couldn't quite ignore what they said.

"The police are completely baffled," exclaimed Gwen, the businesswoman in a soft gray suit. "Their detectives have no clue where the murder happened."

"Probably not," replied Christine who was wearing a blue blazer and tan slacks in the colors of the vehicle leasing company she managed out in the industrial park. "I heard that Mister Johnston had been shot twice and his body dumped in the river. A driver's license in his pocket allowed the police to identify the body, but there are so many miles of river bank, plus several bridges to check out, that they may never discover where he was killed."

"And to think," said Gwen, "just yesterday morning, some of my employees were cleaning Mister Johnston's condo. I stopped by to hurry them up because my Lucky Ladies Cleaning Service is swamped with work these days, and we had several other residences to clean. In any case, the girls were running late and hadn't started yet when I walked through the door."

Christine shivered. "You cleaned a dead man's condo?"

"Yes, but we didn't know he was dead at the time."

"What did his place look like inside?"

Rita leaned forward in order not to miss a single word. She'd never heard real live details about a homicide before, and this was definitely more intriguing than the meeting.

"Well, we always clean his place on Mondays," said Gwen. "And last week we gave it an extra good cleaning because I was breaking in some new help and wanted to get them off on the right foot. But this Monday, since the place looked scarcely touched from the week before, I told the girls to just hit the high spots and move on."

"You didn't have to do much then?"

"The only obvious cleanup was the dead flowers in a vase on top of the narrow sofa table in front of the window. The flowers were fresh cut blossoms one week and dried up brown stalks the next. I threw them in a trash bag and washed the cut-glass vase out in the sink. The girls vacuumed up the dried flower petals that had fallen onto the windowsill, plus all those on top of the table."

"Nice furniture?"

"Let me tell you, that is a nice sofa table. It's made out of cherry wood. I'd like to have one like that. Anyway, the Persian carpet under the edge of the table looked as clean as the day he bought it, so I told the girls to skip the rug and move on. I'd say we were done in an hour or so, which pretty much put us back on schedule."

"Don't suppose you found anything interesting in his condo?"

"We didn't find any bodies or blood, if that's what you mean." Gwen put her hand on Christine's sleeve. "Now tell me what you know."

Rita leaned as close as she could without becoming obvious.

"The police came by my office yesterday afternoon," said Christine, "shortly after they found the body. It seems the SUV Mister Johnston leased from us had been towed to the city lot a few days ago as an abandoned vehicle because it had been parked on the same street too long."

"Why didn't the police notify you when it was towed?"

"That's what I asked them and they said they were notifying me now."

"Oh, my" said Gwen. "Well, did you go look at the vehicle?"

"I did," replied Christine. "The evidence techs were going through the SUV, so I couldn't touch anything. I peeked through all the windows and nothing seemed out of place. No damage to the outside and none that I could see to the inside. Of course, the rear seats were folded flat, so I'll have to wait until later to see if the rear leather seats or the floorboards have any damage there."

"No bodies or blood?" teased Gwen.

Rita was close enough to see one of Christine's eyebrows arch upward.

"No," said Christine, "only a few letters from over the sun visor. The envelopes had Mister Johnston's name on them and that's how the police connected him to the vehicle. I identified the SUV and confirmed the lease. Now you know as much about the murder as I do. We may never know where he was killed."

At this point Rita could contain herself no longer. "I think you ought to call the police right away and tell them what you know about the murder site."

QUESTION: Who was Rita talking to, where was the murder site, and what was the clue that tipped off Rita?

SOLUTION: Rita was talking to Gwen of the Lucky Ladies Cleaning Service because Mr. Johnston had been shot in his condo while on the Persian carpet. Dead flower petals had fallen on top of the narrow sofa table and as far out as the windowsill, therefore petals should also have fallen on the Persian carpet, but Gwen said the carpet was as clean as the day he bought it. Since the body was already on the rug, and blood is hard to remove from fabric, the killers merely rolled up the body and like a magician using deception to accomplish a trick, they gave him a magic carpet ride out of the building, probably into the SUV, and then later replaced the carpet with a similar one.

THE BIG BUILD UP

Rita hadn't meant to overhear the conversation on the other side of the corner end table where magazines were laid out for patients in the doctor's waiting room; it was just that the two women were whispering so loud.

"Michael has the face of a movie star," exclaimed the well-dressed lady with diamond rings on both hands. "And you should see his build. Well, maybe you shouldn't, I really don't need any competition."

"Oh Dana, I'm already happily married," said her friend Kari. "Besides, it's nice you found someone else. Hank's been gone what, three years now?"

Rita turned a page in her magazine and tried to concentrate on the article. She hoped Dana would lower her voice, but it didn't happen that way.

"Actually, it's been two and a half years," replied Dana in the same loud whisper.

"Then it's about time you had some romance in your life," said Kari. "So, tell me all about Michael."

"He says he's a venture capitalist from California."

"Sounds exciting, but what exactly does he do?"

Dana took a deep breath. "Well, he's starting up a small business in Mexico. It won't be much at first, but as his product becomes better known, he will acquire new investors and expand the factory."

"Why Mexico?"

"You know how bureaucratic our federal agencies can be with a new idea. But in the meantime, Michael can make his product in Mexico and sell it down there for lots of money while he's waiting for the Food and Drug Administration to approve his application up here."

By now, Rita had given up reading the article. The whispering was too much of a distraction, especially since Kari kept asking questions about the new boyfriend.

"What sort of product is it?"

Now the whispering dropped to a lower volume as Dana leaned closer to her friend.

"Michael's invented a new protein powder that grows muscles in a matter of months."

"You mean like all these baseball players on steroids?"

Dana shook her head. "No steroids in this formula, but it works just as fast or faster. And Michael's formula is a lot safer."

Rita bent down the upper corner of her magazine and glanced over the top in time to see Kari frown.

"How do you know it works?" asked Kari.

"I've seen his muscles. Yesterday, Michael took me to the spa where he lifts weights and does exercises on various machines." At this point in the conversation, Dana gave a grin that was almost wicked. "He looks really great in nylon jogging shorts and a tight-fitting t-shirt with the sleeves cut off."

"Go on, don't stop now," exclaimed Kari.

"Well," said Dana, "I was watching him go through his workout when this man in gym clothes stepped up beside me and asked if I knew Michael."

"Who was the man?"

"Some member of the spa. Turns out the man had watched Michael grow from a very slender build to having a muscular one almost like Arnold Swartzenegger. And Michael did it in only three months. The spa member is now one of Michael's investors. That proves the formula works. I just hope the Food and Drug Administration will hurry up and approve Michael's application so he can cash in on his new protein invention."

Kari sighed. "You are one lucky girl. What are your future plans?"

"Michael's kind of broke right now. All of his money is invested in his new formula. He takes me out for pizza instead of lobster, but he says that will all change after the factory in Mexico starts up production."

"Pizza?" inquired Kari. "Then you haven't introduced Michael to your country club friends?"

Dana made a face. "Not yet. I plan to in the very near future, but I think I had better buy him some new business suits first so he looks really nice when I present him to that group."

"What's wrong with the clothes he wears now? You said he looks good."

"Oh, he does. His suits show him off quite well, it's just that..."

"What?"

"Well, his suits fit him very well, but they're at least three or four years out of date. If he's going to impress my friends, he needs more stylish clothing."

"Good point," replied Kari. She was then in the process of recommending a certain high-class men's stores with the latest styles, when a nurse stepped out into the waiting room and called Dana's name.

Rita lowered the top of her magazine and watched Dana say goodbye to her friend. The well-dressed woman with two diamond rings then followed the nurse down the hall and out of sight. Kari, still waiting for her name to be called, picked up a health magazine from the end table and began leafing through the pages.

Now, Rita had a problem. She didn't want to be accused of eavesdropping, but she also didn't want Michael to take advantage of unsuspecting Dana. Oh well, she'd never see these two women again, but on the other hand, she definitely wouldn't feel right if she didn't at least give a warning.

Closing the magazine and placing it in her lap, Rita cleared her throat until Kari looked up at her. "I hope your friend doesn't invest in Michael's new formula."

"Excuse me," replied Kari.

"Michael is a fraud," said Rita. "Advise Dana not to give him any money at all."

Then a nurse called Rita's name. She put her magazine back on the end table and left Kari with an open mouth.

QUESTION: How did Rita know that Michael was a scam artist?

SOLUTION: If Michael had grown a large muscular build in just three months, then his three to four-year-old suits would not have fit him anymore. Obviously, the stranger at the spa who vouched for Michael was an accomplice in the scam, and Michael will soon ask Dana for money.

THE POISON PEN LETTER

Vice Detective Oscar had just been promoted to the city's Homicide Squad, but wasn't sure this was the job he wanted to be working in law enforcement. It was one thing to go undercover proactively and try to outwit criminals in a vice sting or a drug buy, and quite something else to find himself staring at one of the recently deceased while trying to figure out what had happened after the fact. He could tell real quick that this type of law enforcement work could be a real headache. With a quiet sigh, he kept his hands in the front pockets of his coat and out of the way.

"I was the first cop on the scene," said Corporal Davis, "and nothing's been touched since I got here." He used his left thumb to indicate a body seated in an office chair, while the body's shoulders and head rested on top of a large desk. There was a small round hole in the right temple of the victim.

"And this," continued the corporal as he waved a hand at a fidgety civilian on the other side of the desk, "is Mister Brewer, the deceased's business partner."

Detective Oscar barely looked at Brewer before returning his attention to Corporal Davis.

"Anything to go on?" he inquired.

"Looks like he was writing a letter at the time of the shooting," replied the corporal. He then pointed out a sheet of paper lying close to the victim's right hand, plus a nearby ball point pen.

Oscar leaned over to glance at the letter written in cursive. Most of it was easily readable.

"From the contents of this document," Corporal Davis said, "it appears that the victim had an ongoing argument with one of his subcontractors whom he's accusing of ripping off the company, but if you notice how there's an irregular line running down from the last letter of what seems to be an unfinished name, I'd suggest that the victim didn't get to finish writing."

"How much of the unfinished name do we have," asked Oscar.

"The first name is Bryan," replied the corporal as he bent over the note, "but we only got a T-H-O- for the last name."

"That would be Bryan Thornton," interjected Mr. Brewer at the head of the desk. His hands twitched nervously as he spoke. "My partner and I have had a lot of trouble with him lately, but I didn't think it would go this far."

"Where can we find this Bryan?" asked Detective Oscar.

"No problem," Mr. Brewer managed to squeak out. Then before anyone could stop him, he grabbed a small note pad off the top of the desk plus the ball point pen lying near the victim's hand. He clicked the top of the pen and commenced to print out Bryan's name and address in black ink letters.

The corporal's mouth dropped open in shock. "Put that down, Mister Brewer," he commanded in a loud voice. "That letter may help implicate Bryan Thornton as the murderer, and you're interfering with our evidence."

Detective Oscar studied Mr. Brewer for a thoughtful moment.

"You're partially right, corporal," he finally said. "Mister Brewer is interfering with our evidence, but I scarcely think his deceased business partner wrote that letter in the first place."

QUESTION: What makes newly made Homicide Detective Oscar believe that the deceased business partner did not write the letter which appears to incriminate subcontractor Bryan Thornton?

SOLUTION: If the victim was writing the letter at the time of the shooting, as the line of ink trailing off from the unfinished name seems to indicate, then the ball point would still be extended outside the pen for writing. However, when Mr. Brewer unthinkingly picked up the pen to write down Bryan's name and address, he had to first click the top of the pen to extend the ball point into a writing position. After shooting the victim, the killer had obviously forged the letter as a red herring to cast suspicion on Bryan and then staged the letter and pen near the body. And, like a lot of people, when he was done writing, the killer clicked the pen closed.

THE HOLE TRUTH

The defendant, Jazz Yarnell, had just taken the witness stand in his own defense against the charge of accessory to homicide during a burglary. His attorney quickly led him through the basic facts leading up to the shooting and ended with how bad Jazz felt when he later discovered his partner in crime had shot an off-duty cop. Then his attorney sat down.

"Any cross examination?" inquired the judge.

Jen, the assistant county prosecutor, had been led by opposing counsel, right up until the previous thirty minutes, to believe the defense attorney's client would not take the stand under any conditions. Surprised by this reversal and due to a heavy case load, she found herself not as well prepared for this witness as she would like to have been. With several different thoughts vying for attention in her mind, she stood for cross. Now she would just have to wing it.

"Mister Yarnell, you and your partner, a Mister Beaumont, were leaving the rear exit of a sporting goods store at one o'clock in the morning. Correct?"

"We were behind the sporting goods store, yeah, but I wouldn't necessarily say we had been inside that store."

Jen repressed a smile.

"Okay, we'll come back to the burglary part later. Now, as the two of you stepped out into the alley, you were confronted by a man in civilian clothes, the same type of clothes as you or any other man might wear these days?"

"Right, the guy was not wearing a uniform or anything to let us know he was a cop."

"And you said in your testimony here today that the man confronting you did not show a badge?

"He didn't show us nothing."

Jen consulted a white paper document, plus some handwritten notes on her yellow legal pad before her next question.

"Even though officers responding to the scene later reported the off-duty officer, or the guy as you refer to him, had his badge on a chain around his neck and the badge was on top of his jacket?"

"It was a little dark in that alley, but we didn't see nothing like a badge."

"And you also claim the man in the alley did not announce himself as being a policeman?"

Right, he didn't say a thing."

Jen made a check mark on her legal pad.

"To move on, Mister Yarnell, you further stated in your testimony that the off-duty officer fired first and your partner only shot back in self-defense?"

"Yeah. The guy shot at us first. We didn't know if he was some kind of vigilante out there trying to get his moment of fame in the newspapers, or maybe even a serial killer shooting people at random. That happens, you know, just look at the news. A guy's got to be careful these days, so Beaumont shot back."

Jen continued.

"Shell casings found at the scene show that your Mister Beaumont fired his automatic pistol twice. The off-duty officer's revolver had one discharged cartridge in the cylinder. That makes three shots total."

"Could be, I was trying to duck behind a dumpster after the shooting started, so I didn't keep track."

"Your partner, this Mister Beaumont, took one round to the heart and expired immediately. The off-duty officer was severely wounded with one round, and the third bullet was found in a telephone pole down the alley."

"Like I said, I was just trying to get out of the way. I wasn't paying any attention to where shots were going."

"But you had no gun?"

"Right."

"And you didn't pull any trigger?"

"Correct, I didn't shoot anybody. My fingerprints were not found on any of the guns, and tests showed there was no powder residue on me or any of my clothes."

Jen hugged her yellow legal pad of notes lightly to her chest with crossed arms.

"I believe you Mister Yarnell when you say you didn't fire a shot. But I'm sure your defense attorney has explained to you that any homicide committed during a felony makes you responsible as an accessory to that homicide?"

"He explained it all to me, but this was self-defense. The guy shot first without saying anything to us. We didn't know who he was."

"I assume your attorney also told you the off-duty officer died later without regaining consciousness?"

"He happened to mention that."

"So, out of three people in that alley that night, you are the only survivor. The only one to come out alive. You can tell your story any way you want."

Yarnell's face acquired a barely concealed grin.

"Like I said, I didn't shoot anybody, and it was self-defense on Beaumont's part. The cop should've showed us a badge or said something instead of shooting. We'd have surrendered peaceably."

"Go ahead and smile if you like, Mister Yarnell, but your shooting story has a hole in it, a hole which will send you straight to prison as an accessory to homicide."

QUESTION: Where is the hole in Yarnell's story?

SOLUTION: The crime scene showed that the off-duty policeman only fired one round, while Beaumont shot twice. If Beaumont died immediately from being shot in the heart, then Beaumont had to have fired his weapon first, and done it twice. Therefore, the off-duty officer could not have shot first. This is no self-defense from an allegedly unknown stranger in the alley. Yarnell is making up a story to his best advantage.

THE RIGHT TRACK

As a railroad detective, J.C. McCord had worked petty theft cases, removed an unruly passenger or two, and even apprehended a con man plying his trade on the rail line, but this was her first case of a passenger leaving the train while it was still in motion. Looking forward to a challenge, she boarded the Amtrak in Grand Junction, almost at the western border of Colorado, and sat down with the only witness to the incident. Time was short before the train moved on.

"Mister Pitt, I'm Detective McCord. I understand you knew the deceased."

"I didn't exactly know him, we met here in the dining car. He was sitting by himself and I wasn't traveling with anyone so I sat down at his table."

"You joined him?"

"Yes, to have some company while I ate."

J.C. jotted down some notes. "Go on."

"At first, he didn't make much sense, wanted to know if I'd ever been to South America. I told him no.

Then he said this might be a good time for him to go somewhere, get away from the world for a while."

"What was your reply?"

"Lots of people say those things at one time or another, so I agreed just to keep the conversation going. Later, he mentioned that he was traveling from Denver to California."

"Did he give a reason for his travel?"

Pitt nodded.

"After a couple of drinks, Mister Albert really loosened up, told me more than I wanted to know."

J.C. paused in her writing. "Such as?"

"Said he and his accounting records were being subpoenaed to federal court in California on a corporation embezzlement scandal. He even tapped his index finger on the briefcase he was carrying to indicate the records were right there with him. Seems he was part of the scheme and was supposed to testify against upper management. In return, the feds cut him a deal for minimum jail time."

"How did he feel about all that?"

Pitt rubbed his chin.

"Mostly depressed. Made comments about how nice it would be if this were somehow over and done with."

J.C. waited, pen poised.

"And then?"

"We talked until he seemed to be in a better frame of mind. Then he left for his sleeping compartment."

"No problems at that point?"

"Not that I saw. Later, I left the dining car, and there Albert was, between cars with the south door open to the outside. It didn't look good to me."

"What did you do?"

"I asked what was going on. He said he was going to

end it all."

J.C. looked up.

Pitt continued.

"He threw his briefcase out the door and then he jumped. It happened too fast to stop him."

J.C. started to form another question, but her cell phone interrupted. She glanced at Caller ID, the local sheriff's department.

"J.C. here." Then she repeated the cell phone conversation aloud as she added to her notes.

"You say your deputies came in from the west and discovered Mister Albert's body roughly where the witness said it would be on the south side of the tracks. What about a briefcase?"

She began to write again.

"Deputies found the briefcase first, so knew they were in the right area. Okay. Anything in the briefcase?"

J.C. paused.

"Nothing? But you say the latch was broken and strong winds might have blown any papers away, probably well scattered by now. No, that's fine, I think that's all I need."

She closed her cell phone.

"One more item, Mister Pitt. Why were you traveling on this train."

QUESTION: Why should Detective J.C. McCord be suspicious of Pitt's statements, or is Pitt's story on the right track?

SOLUTION: The Amtrak was west bound from Denver to California, so if Albert threw his briefcase from the train before he jumped then the briefcase should have been located east of his body. But, according to the Sheriff's Department, the deputies coming in from the west found the briefcase first. Since Pitt is the sole witness, he likely grabbed the briefcase, pushed Albert off the train, took the incriminating documents, then tossed the briefcase and tried to make the situation appear to be suicide.

TIRED

R ita couldn't help overhearing the conversation in the restaurant booth behind her. Not that she was eavesdropping on purpose, but the voices of the three women tourists did carry plainly over the back of the booth.

It had been Rita's original intention to have a quiet leisurely breakfast at a restaurant located near the interstate, before she headed downtown to attend the annual conference for local businesswomen. Now it looked like the quiet part of breakfast was not to be. But at least the coffee was served hot and aromatic. Selecting a small, white-plastic container of cream, she dribbled its contents into her cup while the conversation of the three ladies wrapped around her.

Two elderly women travelers, Wilma and Leona, from out of state, were counting their blessings over the Good Samaritan they'd been lucky enough to find when their car developed troubles during their tour of the local countryside. A third lady, Mary, sat quietly in the booth as Wilma and Leona each competed to tell the story first.

"It was a good thing Wilma was the one driving on that back-country road yesterday afternoon. I don't know if I could've controlled the car when those tires went flat."

"Believe me," said Wilma, "my hands were glued to the steering wheel. I don't ever want to go through something like that again. We just missed wiping out the speed limit sign and we weren't even speeding."

"Nails in both front tires," exclaimed Leona. "It's a wonder we didn't crash."

Rita sipped her coffee and mused to herself that she didn't really believe in luck, but sometimes strange things did happen.

"I'll tell you where else we were fortunate," replied Wilma, "when that pickup truck stopped to see if we needed help. But us with two flat tires and only one spare, all that man could do was give us the telephone number of the garage in the next town down the road. I telephoned the garage and that nice Wilbur Jones answered. He turned out to be our Good Samaritan."

"Three miles to the nearest town," said Leona, "I couldn't have walked that far. I can see I better get me a cell phone like yours if we're going to take any more trips across the country."

Barely waiting until Leona had finished talking, Wilma made her next statement. "All I said to Mister Jones was that we had two flat tires, and then described where our car was located. He said he was with a customer at the time, but would be out as soon as he could throw a couple of tires into the back of his tow truck."

Rita wasn't sure the two ladies were totally listening to what the other one had said, but they did seem to pick up at least part of the other woman's statement and base their reply on those few words. The third woman, Mary, scarcely had a chance to speak.

"We only had to wait a half hour," Leona said.

"I saw that white tow truck coming down the road and I knew it was Mister Jones," added Wilma.

"And he had two tires already mounted on rims," continued Leona. "He said the tires and rims had been ordered last month by a customer, but the fellow never picked them up. Imagine that. Of course, it being a small town and all, we had to pay top price for the tires and a little extra for the rims, but like Mister Jones told us, we can always use the original set of rims to mount snow tires on. That way it will save us time and money when changing tires every spring and fall."

"A very helpful and considerate man," said Wilma.

"Yes," agreed Leona, "and it was nice of his wife to send along that thermos of hot coffee and those delicious blueberry muffins she'd just made. Both of us were so tired and worn out by the entire ordeal, yet we got to sit comfortably in our car while Mister Jones changed the tires by himself and put the two flats in the trunk."

Rita took another sip of her own coffee and thought about the two flat tires on rims in the trunk of the ladies' car.

"We'll probably never tour this part of the country again," said Wilma, "but it is nice to know there are some Good Samaritans out there willing to help out-of-state people like us. I tell you, Mary, we were very, very fortunate."

"Here's to Mister Jones, and good luck in the future while traveling," replied Leona.

"You two were very lucky indeed," Mary finally

managed to insert into the conversation.

Rita turned around and looked over the back of the booth in time to see Wilma and Leona raising their coffee cups in a toast to their Good Samaritan.

"Excuse me," said Rita, "but if I were you, I would notify the Better Business Bureau so nobody else gets ripped off."

QUESTION: What was Rita's clue that something was wrong?

SOLUTION: All Wilma told Mister Jones was that they had two flat tires, plus the location of their car. Since Wilma did not mention the make of their car, how did Mister Jones know the size of tires they needed? Evidently, the garage owner had an accomplice stationed near that back-country road to scatter a few nails on the asphalt whenever he saw an out-of-state vehicle coming in their direction. The accomplice, probably the driver of the pickup truck that stopped to ask if they needed help, could then phone ahead to the garage with a description of the car, thus Mr. Jones could be prepared to skin a couple of unwary tourists.

TOO TALL TOM

B eing a claims adjuster for a major insurance company, Molly had a nose for fraud, and as she walked up the sidewalk toward their client's wooden two-story house, her senses started tingling. Carefully, she skirted the mountain bike leaning against the concrete stoop and stepped up onto the porch. Before she could ring the front doorbell, a tall man suddenly appeared on the other side of the screen door.

"Mister Johnston?" she inquired.

"That's me," replied the man.

Molly quickly identified herself and was invited into the house. In the living room, she chose to sit at one end of the brass-studded Moroccan couch where she had use of the coffee table to lay out her paperwork.

"Just call me Tom," said the man as he sat back in the easy chair across the room. He moved with the easy grace of an athlete.

"Very well…Tom. We need to fill out the claim form on your wrecked vehicle. I see the title is in the names of both you and your wife, and our insurance policy covers the car."

"Correct."

"You said on the phone that your vehicle was wrecked last night?"

"Right, it was a one car accident without damage to other property. Our vehicle sustained the only injury, but it was still drivable and my wife needed to get home right away, so she drove it straight here and no one's touched it since."

Molly paused at the next line on the claim form.

"What was her hurry?"

"She had to pack for a last-minute business conference out of town. Barely made it to the gate in time for her airplane flight."

"How did she get to the airport?"

"I called a cab for her."

Molly shuffled through the paper work until she stopped at a certain document.

"And how have you been getting around these days?"

Tom grinned.

"If my wife's available, then she drives me wherever I need to go. Other than that, well, you noticed the mountain bike leaning against the front porch? And, as slow as it goes, I haven't gotten any more speeding tickets."

Molly put the document she was holding back into the stack of papers.

"It's nice to know you're aware that any use of the vehicle by yourself would violate your insurance policy."

"Oh yes, I'm very conscientious on that point, so I stick to my bicycle for transportation until I get my suspended driver's license back from the state."

Molly rolled the ball point pen between her fingers. "When can I speak with your wife Bev? I need some information from her."

At that moment, Mr. Johnston's cell phone rang.

"Excuse me," he said. He picked up the phone and walked into the next room.

Molly only caught fragments of the conversation. To occupy her time, she glanced around the living room, trying to draw a mental picture of the Johnston's. High-end furniture, a couple of oil paintings on the walls, expensive Persian carpets on the floor and three framed photos on an end table. She took a closer look.

In one photo, Tom posed on a charter boat with a prize Marlin he'd evidently just landed; in another, Bev stood smiling with a tennis racquet held ready in the backhand position; and in the third, with a tropical sunset in the background, Bev stood up on tiptoe to give Tom a peck on the cheek. It appeared that Tom had leaned over so she could reach him more easily.

"Very considerate of him," mused Molly. "They seem to be a very active and loving couple, so why am I suspicious?"

Tom finished his phone call and returned to the living room.

"Where were we?"

"I need to speak with your wife," replied Molly.

"Right," said Tom. "I'll have her call you at your office tomorrow as soon as she gets back and you two can talk on the phone. Is that okay?"

"It will have to do." Molly gathered up her papers. "Shall we go look at the car?"

"Sure, it's right out in the garage where Bev left it."

Tom led the way.

Molly ran her fingers over the crumpled right front

fender. Pieces of fender metal had been bent almost down to the front passenger tire.

"Bev mentioned something about loose gravel throwing the car off the road," said Tom. I think the fender must've scraped a large rock when it went in the ditch."

"I see," replied Molly. "May I look at your registration papers? I need to compare the VIN to our policy."

"Not a problem." Tom opened the driver's door and slid easily onto the leather seat behind the steering wheel. He pulled down the sun visor and extracted some documents from a pouch.

Molly checked the numbers against her paperwork and handed back the registration documents.

"Everything should be in order," said Tom, "so after my wife calls you, we'll expect a check from the company to cover the cost of repairs."

Molly smiled politely, but it was her intention to confront Tom's wife in person, not over the phone. If her interview with Bev was as successful as Molly thought it would be, then the insurance company wouldn't have to pay a dime.

QUESTION: What tipped Molly off to this probable case of fraud?

SOLUTION: Tom was such a tall man that Bev had to stand on tiptoe to kiss his cheek. He even had to lean over so she could reach him. But when Tom slid into the driver's seat of their damaged vehicle to get the registration, he did it easily, which meant he had been the last one to drive the vehicle, not his shorter wife. Tom was setting Bev up to take the blame, since he had no valid driver's license.

WHERE THERE'S FIRE

As a new Deputy, Makenzie knew she'd have to be careful if she wanted to keep her job. This was election year with a close race for the Sheriff's position. Normally, her boss ensured all department investigations were conducted without regard to politics, but recently he had made it very clear there would be no incidents reflecting badly on his department. If the deputies were correct in their investigative decisions then fine, he'd back them. But if they made a mistake in judgment, then...

Makenzie understood his situation, but that didn't help her now. Earlier this evening, she had responded to a simple call of vandalism, a minor crime the shift sergeant believed safe enough for a "newbie" to pursue on her own. Unfortunately, the main suspect was nineteen-year-old "Sonny" DeMarte, sole offspring of the County Commissioner.

As Makenzie pulled her Sheriff's Department SUV into the DeMarte driveway, she was relieved to see the Commissioner's car was absent from his residence.

She slid out of the driver's seat as dead leaves skittered across the cement, pushed by early autumn breezes. Front porch lights showed the only vehicle present belonged to the main suspect. She rang the doorbell.

Sonny answered the door. "What can I do for you, Deputy?"

Makenzie decided to low key it. "May I come in?"

Sonny stepped aside, closing the door behind her.

In the living room, Makenzie found two more of the DeMarte clan, teenage male cousins of Sonny. They stared and waited to see what she wanted.

"I'm investigating some reported vandalism."

Sonny spread his hands, palms outward. "Wasn't me, I've been here all night."

"And," piped up one of the cousins, "we'll vouch for him."

Makenzie smiled. "I didn't say when this incident occurred."

Sonny grinned back mischievously. "Then let us in on when and I'll see if I can scare up an alibi."

Keeping a friendly tone, Makenzie replied, "Just tell me where you've been for the last two hours."

Sonny glanced at his two cousins. "I sat right here watching television all evening."

Makenzie fixed Sonny's current appearance in her mind. Hiking boots, blue jeans, wool long-sleeved shirt, long brown hair and a ball cap with a fishing logo. No coat in sight.

"I suppose you could tell me about the shows you watched?"

Sonny's grin got bigger. "Sure could." He went on to talk about sitcom characters and their funny scenes.

Makenzie quickly figured out these sitcoms were reruns which Sonny could have seen during their premier showing. He could've even acquired his information from the local television guide. Not much of a convincing alibi.

"I don't suppose you helped build the bonfire at the Kramer place out along the river tonight?" she inquired.

"Bonfire? Not me. Why, what happened?"

"Whoever had a party around the bonfire also painted graffiti on the house. Seems the Kramers came home early, which broke up the party."

"Anybody say I was there?" asked Sonny.

"Mister Kramer says a vehicle leaving the property looked like yours. You know, the car setting out in the driveway."

"Well, unless he wrote down a license plate number, Kramer will have a tough time proving my car was there. Did he get a plate number?"

Makenzie ignored the question. Instead, she continued pressing, looking for a crack in Sonny's story. "Mister Kramer also reported one of the bonfire partiers was wearing a long sleeve wool shirt exactly like the one you have on right now."

Sonny shrugged.

"C'mon, deputy, there must be a dozen guys in this county with a shirt just like mine. Half the stores in town sell them, so what does that prove?"

"You're probably correct on that point, Sonny."

Makenzie stepped closer to her suspect. "However, there is one quick way to determine if you were at that bonfire tonight."

QUESTION: What simple test can Deputy Makenzie immediately conduct to determine whether Sonny might have been at the bonfire instead of at home like he said?

SOLUTION: Makenzie should get close enough to check out Sonny's shirt, because the wool cloth would smell of wood smoke if he had been out at the campfire instead of at home watching television all night as he claimed to be.

TRACKED DOWN

"Nicky, we've got a real bad problem out on the beach."

Driving with her left hand and reaching for the handset with her right, Nicky concentrated on the incoming radio call. She'd been a Ranger in the Coastal Dunes Park for three years now, but most of the problems had resulted in nothing more than loud parties, littered campsites, or dogs running loose without owners nearby. This time it sounded serious. She grabbed the handset off the console and pushed the send button.

"This is Nicky. Go ahead."

"Meet a Mister John Landrigan at the pull-off near mile marker 46. He's there on a black motorcycle."

"Sure, what's going on?"

"Mister Landrigan was setting up his camera equipment to take some commercial shots of the ocean over the sand dunes. When he turned his back to get a light meter out of his saddlebags, he heard a vehicle drive along the beach front. It stopped for a minute, and then took off in a hurry. By the time he got back to his camera for the photo, he saw a body lying on the sand not far from the water. He claims not to have heard any sounds other than the noise of the engine and maybe a vehicle door slamming."

"Okay, I'm on my way."

"Anything you want me to do back here at base?"

Nicky thought for a moment. This was the off season and it had been raining up until this morning. There couldn't be very many tourists and vehicles in the park yet. She clicked the send button again.

"Yes, call the north and south gates. Tell them not to let in any more tourists until we get this figured out. And tell them to hold all vehicles trying to leave the park."

"Will do. Where will you be if I need you?"

"I'll meet with the witness, check out the situation and get back to you on the radio as soon as possible."

Five minutes later, Nicky pulled off the road and parked at mile marker 46. She met with Mister Landrigan, and then walked down through the sand dunes toward the beach to observe the body for herself. Careful to stay several feet back from the crime scene, Nicky took notes on her flip top spiral notebook.

A body lay on its back between a set of tire tracks in the sand. One arm, the right arm, stretched straight out from the body, its hand resting across the top of one line of the tire tracks. Nikky took a step in and looked closer. There was a round hole in the front of the victim's jacket. Obvious gunshot. But it was also obvious from the lack of footprints that the victim hadn't walked to this spot on the beach.

After making a large clockwise circle around the crime scene, Nikky realized there were no tracks in the beach sand other than the ones she had made, plus the tire tracks made by one vehicle. Earlier long days of rain had smoothed the sand so that any traffic on the beach previous to this morning had gradually been obliterated. Now, all the evidence contained within the circle she'd made consisted only of the body and the tire tracks. Returning to her Park Ranger vehicle, Nikky leaned in and keyed the mike.

"Base from Nikky."

"This is base, go ahead."

"How many vehicles have entered the park today?"

"Four. One belongs to the witness, Mister Landrigan. Of the other three, two of the vehicles are being held at the South Gate and one's now stopped at the North Gate."

"How many people in each vehicle?"

"There's one person in each, just the driver. And the gate guards only remember seeing one person sitting in each vehicle when they drove in."

"What types of vehicles are these three?"

"Well, there's a blue four door sedan that's a couple of years old, a brand-new red pickup truck that's still got a paper plate in the window and there's a green van like the type they deliver flowers in. Why?"

Sitting sideways in the driver's seat with the door propped open, Nikky idly tapped her fingers on the steering wheel as she considered her options. Only three vehicles other than the witness. She quickly discounted the witness and his vehicle because the gate guards would have easily noticed a passenger, either dead or alive, on the back of his motorcycle. No, it had to be one of the other three, but which one?

Two minutes later, the corners of her mouth turned up in a grim smile. Clicking the send button once more,

Nikky gave instructions to the gate guards.

QUESTION: Which vehicle and driver did Nikky want the gate guards to pay special attention to and why?

SOLUTION: To not leave his own footprints, the driver of the four-door sedan would have pushed or pulled the body out to the side of the tire tracks, not into the center of the tracks, so count him out. And, the driver of the pickup would have to get out of the truck in order to remove any body covered up in the truck bed, and therefore would have left footprints in the sand even if he was able to roll the victim out the back and into the center of the tire tracks. That leaves the driver of the delivery van who had only to move inside to the rear door, open it and push the body out the back right into the center of both tire tracks.

WHERE'D HE GO?

Detective Sergeant Henry Stanton put one hand up against the brick wall of the nearest building, bent over and tried to get his breath back. It was on his mind that he was getting too old to be chasing these young purse snatchers on foot. Sure, he'd run track in high school, but that was years ago and he hadn't been wearing street shoes back then. It also seemed that maybe thieves were getting faster these days.

Two more short breaths, then he straightened up and stepped around the corner into the alley. Nobody in sight at this point, but he wasn't too surprised. Henry moved a little way into the broken asphalt corridor before stopping to rest again. This time, he carefully sat back on the third rung up of a metal extension ladder which leaned against the side of a one-story building to his right. From several sealed buckets and a black-tarred mop stacked nearby, he figured some roofers must've temporarily left the ladder in place when their work was interrupted by a recent heavy rain. They'd probably be back later to finish the job and retrieve their equipment.

Farther down the alley, he noticed dumpsters, trash cans, tall piles of debris and a few back doors which were probably locked to any outside entry, unless of course that person had a key. A third brick building sealed off the corridor's other exit. Henry quickly realized this formed a dead end with no way out for the thief.

Picking up a small stick near the bottom of the ladder, Henry proceeded to pry heavy mud off the sole of his right shoe. All this weight was slowing him down and making it more difficult for him to move. Luckily, he hadn't slipped and fallen when the chase crossed a vacant lot filled with weeds and thick, wet soil. He inspected the right pant leg of his brand-new suit and brushed off a few flakes of drying dirt. Didn't look like the suit would have to go to the cleaners. He could probably just wipe off any spots on the cuffs with a damp rag when he got back to the station.

By the time Henry got to prying mud off the sole of his left shoe, two uniformed policeman drove up in a black and white. They stepped quickly out of their squad car and into the alley. Both had their guns drawn and ready.

"Where'd he go, Sarge?" asked the older patrolman. "We saw you follow him in here. Did you see where he went after that?"

Henry shook his head. "Nope, I was too far behind him. He disappeared before I got around the corner, but it's a dead end so you can probably find him hiding in there somewhere." Henry stood up and away from the ladder. He waved one hand toward the dumpsters and stacks of debris at the far end.

The older patrolman started moving slowly into the

alley, checking out potential hiding places as he went.

"I'll check the roof in case he went that way," said the younger patrolman as he put one hand on a metal rung and prepared to climb.

"Don't bother," Henry replied. "The thief is still down here in the alley."

QUESTION: Why does Detective Sergeant Henry Stanton believe that the fugitive purse snatcher is still in the alley instead of trying to escape over the roof?

SOLUTION: With the three brick buildings forming a dead end, the thief had only two choices: over the roof or hide in the alley. Because Henry had to clean the mud off his shoes from the chase through a vacant lot, that meant the thief would have mud on his shoes as well. If the thief had then climbed up the ladder to escape, there would have been mud on the metal rungs. But, Henry sat down on the third rung up in order to clean off his shoes. If there had been mud on the ladder rungs, Henry, worried about getting his brand-new suit dirty, would not have sat down on muddy rungs. Therefore, Henry was sure the thief had to be hiding somewhere in the alley.

YULETIDE TREES

I nsurance Investigator Francine Moore, known as Frankie to her associates, would much rather have been home early to help her family get ready for their usual New Year's Eve party with buttered popcorn, rental movies, silly hats and noisemakers, but business was business. A vehicle accident involving two cars was getting ready for trial, and now she had to interview an eye witness who had suddenly come forward. The witness, one Melvin Carter, claimed to have had a perfect view from the window near his desk in the second story building where he worked.

After introducing herself and displaying her Investigator credentials, Frankie took a seat in the metal office chair on the opposite side of Melvin's desk.

"I understand you saw the accident that happened four months ago in front of your building?"

"That's correct," replied Melvin. "I was sitting right here where I am now and just happened to look out my office window slightly before the crash."

Frankie motioned with her hand. "Do you mind if I

come around to your side so you can show me where the collision took place?"

"Not at all," said Melvin as he pointed his right index finger toward the busy intersection down below. "See, back then, there were two cars stopped in the near lane for a red light, but when the light turned green the first driver must've accidently had his car in reverse because he suddenly rammed backwards into the car behind him. Then after the wreck, he must've gotten the transmission into the right gear because he pulled forward a short ways."

Frankie looked in the direction where Melvin's index finger pointed. She had to admit, it was a clear path of vision from Melvin's desk down to the intersection where the wreck had occurred. True, there was a huge Chestnut tree in the way, but she could plainly see right through the tree's bare branches which the city had strung with bright lights shortly after Thanksgiving.

"Colorful view," said Frankie.

"Yeah," replied Melvin. "Part of the city's effort to bring a little holiday cheer to our downtown area."

"Go on with your story," said Frankie as she walked back to the other side of the desk.

Melvin leaned back in his chair. "Well, there's not much else to tell."

"Was the intersection as busy as it is now?" inquired Frankie.

Melvin shook his head. "No, the streets were pretty quiet then, and I don't remember any pedestrians on the sidewalk. Not at all like these last-minute shopping crowds you see now."

Before continuing, Frankie consulted a claim report filed by the driver of the first car. "Usually in a rear end collision, the party at fault is the one coming from behind. Statistically speaking, they just don't stop in time. And in this case, both vehicles were very expensive, not to mention points being levied against the driver's license of the one at fault."

Melvin spread his hands, palms turned outward. "I saw what I saw."

Frankie closed her file and stood up. "Thank you for your time. It's nice when a citizen decides to come forward as a witness on a case like this."

Melvin merely grinned.

If Frankie hurried, maybe she could still get home in time to help prepare for the family festivities. There was food and beverages to prepare, and since the weeks old decorated spruce tree in the living room was drying out they would need to take it down right after New Year's Eve. Seemed there was always something that needed to be done.

She skipped the crowded elevator and was halfway down the stairs when a thought suddenly occurred to her. "What was Melvin getting out of his pending testimony as a witness? Something was clearly wrong with his version of the collision."

QUESTION: Why is Frankie suspicious of Melvin's story?

SOLUTION: Chestnut trees have very large leaves, and four months earlier when the accident happened, the Chestnut tree should have been in its full leaf coverage. Melvin couldn't have seen anything through the multitude of large leaves, much less which car ran into the other one.

AN ILL WIND

With all the evidence technicians now packed up and headed back to the office, Homicide Detective Jennifer Costa gazed out the open window of the small beachfront house. Out there in the windy sunshine, three young kids ran along the beach at water's edge. Their kites with long tails danced high above the sand dunes. A picturesque and tranquil scene.

Jen felt a twinge of guilt. She'd rather be home spending some time with her own children instead of working all these long hour weeks. After the initial work on this case was finished, maybe she could stop at a store on the way home and pick up a couple of kites.

Shoes scuffling across the floorboards announced the entrance of people behind her.

"Here's the witness you wanted," said one of the junior male detectives. "Her name is Tori Robinson. Says she works here."

Jen paused to watch a seagull run toward the water and launch itself into the air. It took flight and soared. Then Jen turned away from the window to face the distraught young woman.

"You're the one who called the police?" inquired Jen.

"Yes, that's me," replied Tori between sobs. "I work for Mister Kinion. Or I did." A new flood of tears rolled down her smooth cheeks. A faint line of mascara trailed a thin black stripe down the left side.

"I know this is difficult for you right now," Jennifer said with a note of sympathy in her voice, "but I need to ask you some questions."

"Go ahead." Tori sniffed. "I'll do my best."

Detective Costa took out her small notebook.

"What type of work do you do here?"

"I'm a ghost writer for Mister Kinion's manuscripts. He dictates his latest novel into a recorder, then I arrange the words into a readable format."

Jen paused in her note taking long enough to remark, "I believe I've read one or two of his books. Go on."

"We had just finished our novel in time for the publisher's deadline, so I went out to buy a bottle of wine for a little celebration. When I got back, Larry--Mister Kinion that is--was dead on the floor with a pistol in his hand."

"Are you saying it was suicide?"

"Yes, he'd left a note on the table by the open window."

Jen pointed at the window where she had been watching the seagull earlier. "This one?"

"That's correct."

"Sorry, but we didn't find a note. Where is it now?"

"As I told the other detective, it blew out the window, across the beach and right into the ocean. It's gone."

"Well, even if we located it now, the paper would be too waterlogged to read," commented Jen. "But I assume you read the note before it blew away?"

"Yes. Initially, I found Mister Kinion and I couldn't understand why he would do such a thing. This was supposed to be a happy time. Then I saw the note he left and it explained everything. I guess I should've closed the window when I put the note back where I'd found it, but I was more concerned with calling nine-one-one."

"What was in the note?" prompted Jen.

Tori dabbed at her eyes with a tissue.

"There's something I should probably tell you first. During the five years that we worked together, Larry and I gradually fell in love."

"And?" inquired Jen.

"And when I went to the store for the wine, Larry was supposed to call his wife and ask her for a divorce so we could get married," replied Tori.

Jen let the ensuing silence linger as she waited for the rest of the story to come out.

"Larry evidently made the phone call," Tori finally continued after more sobbing, "because he said in the note that his wife refused to give him a divorce. And even worse, now that she knew about us, she was going to ruin him in the publishing world with some information she had from Larry's past. That witch."

"Did Larry say what that information was?"

"No, he just said he'd be ruined as a best-selling author, and therefore suicide was the only way out. Then he apologized to me and signed it 'love, Larry'."

Jen chewed on her lower lip for a moment.

"Did you see anyone else near the house, either when you left or when you returned?"

"After I turned down the dirt road coming back to the beach house, a small red car passed me going in the other direction. Mrs. Kinion drives a red sports car, but I couldn't be sure it was her."

"How long were you gone?"

"At least a couple of hours. I needed to run some other errands while I was out."

"May I see the wine you bought?" asked Jen.

"Sure," replied Tori, "the bottle is right there on the table by the window. It's a Special Reserve Pinot Noir from a California winery Larry and I liked."

Jen removed the wine bottle from the brown paper sack and observed the label.

"I see," said Jen. "This is a very nice touch, but you do realize we have several more questions to be answered before we can close this case."

QUESTION: What led Homicide Detective Jennifer Costa to doubt Larry Kinion's death was a suicide? And if it was murder, then who did she suspect: Tori Robinson or the as yet unseen Mrs. Kinion?

SOLUTION: Since it was a strong wind that day, and seagulls always launch themselves into an available breeze in order to get lift under their wings, the wind was coming from the ocean onto the shore. Any note blowing out of the window would've blown inland, not into the water. In order for Tori Robinson to lie about the note, she must have had a motive. Now it was up to Detective Costa to find out what Tori was hiding and why.

A MATTER OF GLASS

Attorney Katelyn Moore directed her voice to the young man seated on the other side of the conference table. She noticed his designer prescription glasses said a lot about him.

"Mister James, you understand this is a deposition concerning the theft two weeks ago at the private art gallery which you and your partner own?"

James smirked slightly as he used the palm of his right hand to smooth out his brightly colored silk tie which didn't quite go with his blue blazer. Emblazoned in gold on the left breast pocket of his blazer was the art gallery's logo.

"Well, I presumed the theft is why I'm here now."

"You further understand you are under oath to tell the truth, and that everything you and I say will be taken down by the court recorder sitting at the head of the table?"

James glanced at the well-dressed lady moving her fingertips over the keys of a small black machine which fed a long narrow strip of paper in a folding motion onto an attached metal tray. He shrugged.

"I'm ready."

Katelyn continued.

"Our law firm has been retained by the insurance company which has a policy on all contents of your art gallery. Before the insurer pays on the claim filed by you and your partner, we need to establish certain facts."

"Sounds reasonable."

"Good." Katelyn briefly referred to a white sheet of paper in her hand. "According to the police report you were the only one working in the art gallery at the time of the theft. Where was your partner?"

"He was delivering a painting to a buyer several miles up the coast."

"No other employees working that day?"

"Our receptionist took an early lunch. I was alone."

"Where were you when this incident began?"

"I was in the backroom sampling some of the expensive wine which we usually reserve for our better customers. It allows them to relax into a buying mood. We do consider ourselves to be a class establishment, so we offer only the best for our more perceptive clients."

"Of course, then what happened?"

"I had just placed my glasses in the left breast pocket of my blazer when I heard the sound of breaking glass. Therefore, I stepped out into the main gallery."

"And what did you see at this time?"

James visibly inhaled.

"A man in a black ski mask had just smashed the locked glass case where we display our Faberge Egg. Oh, it's not the most intricate of the jeweled Eggs from the Russian Tsar's collection, but it is very expensive none the less. Anyway, broken glass covered the tile floor near the display case....and the thief was placing the jeweled Egg into a small padded pouch."

Katelyn nodded her head in apparent empathy. "What did you do?"

"I shouted at him to stop, but he turned and ran. I couldn't let the thief steal our prized possession, so I tackled him."

"Inside the gallery?"

"Yes, almost at the front doorway."

"And he got away?"

"Yes again, but not without a fight on my part. We rolled across the floor in a violent struggle, even knocked over a couple of vase stands in the process. Finally, he kicked his way loose." James pointed at his left cheek. "The sole of his shoe caught me right here."

"I've seen the police photograph of the abrasion on your cheek," replied Katelyn. "Very brave of you."

"Thank you." James removed his glasses and proceeded to clean them with a special cloth as he spoke. "Are we finished here?"

"Almost." Katelyn glanced up and smiled. "I must admit I've been admiring your designer glasses. May I see them for a moment?"

James responded with his own version of a smile before handing the glasses across the table. "They're just the tiniest bit expensive, but I like them."

Katelyn carefully accepted the slender wire frame in tones of fine gold. "They're much lighter than I expected. As fragile as they appear, you must have them frequently adjusted in order to fit correctly?"

"No, no, I'm very careful with them. In the two months I've owned them, the frames have never needed to be realigned since the day I bought them. Class and good quality always speak for themselves."

Katelyn returned the glasses to their owner.

"And I suppose that since you weren't wearing your glasses at the time, then you won't be able to identify the thief?"

James chuckled. "If you check my prescription, you'll see my distant eye sight isn't really that bad. I wear the glasses mostly for reading, but like I said earlier, the thief was wearing a black ski mask. I couldn't see his face."

Katelyn no longer smiled. She held up her wristwatch.

"Mister James, I'll give you exactly thirty seconds to change your story to the truth, else I'll recommend to my client that you take a polygraph exam about the theft. You now have twenty-five seconds left."

QUESTION: What made Katelyn suspect that Mr. James was lying about the theft?

SOLUTION: If Mr. James had placed his slender designer glasses--the ones with the fragile frames as noted by Katelyn--in the left breast pocket of his blazer before tackling the thief, and if the two men had subsequently rolled across the art gallery's tile floor in a violent struggle as he stated under oath, then the frames of his glasses should have been severely bent. Yet James claimed they had never been adjusted since the day he bought them two months previous. Therefore, the thief may have been James himself, and the cheek wound self-inflicted to bolster his insurance claim.

A QUESTION OF PRINTS

Harry Beltrane opened his bedroom door just enough to listen for movement in the hallway. Nothing. Gradually, he pulled the door wider until there was room for him to slip out into the empty hall. In robe and slippers, he could always claim he was merely looking for a drink of water, should his host or one of the other houseguests inadvertently catch him wandering around in the dark.

Down the wide staircase and onto the expensive Persian carpet in the foyer of the ground floor, he stepped quietly, then turned toward the study. Here he took a pair of thin leather driving gloves out of his left robe pocket, pulled the gloves over his hands and tried the door handle. Unlocked.

Inside the study, Harry walked straight to a large framed canvas hanging behind the home owner's rich mahogany desk. He removed the painting from the wall and stared at the combination lock of a wall safe. Yes, his information had been correct so far.

From the right-side pocket of his robe, Harry

removed a miniature flashlight and a white piece of paper containing a series of numbers. Constantly referring to his notes, he spun the dial one way and then the other until it lined up on the final digit. He cranked the handle. The safe swung open on his first try. Two stacks of money now stared him in the face.

That's when he heard the sound of footsteps in the hall. Someone was coming his way.

Quickly, Harry moved over behind the door and waited.

The door handle turned. Then, one slow step at a time, a man moved into the study.

By the soft moonlight shining in through the window, Harry could tell the man coming in was his host James Mergan, the owner of this large house. What was Mergan thinking? At two o'clock in the morning, the man should have been sleeping in bed, not traipsing around his own study.

"Anybody here?" called the home owner. He tiptoed into the middle of the room, flashlight in hand.

Harry shook his head. This wouldn't do at all. With his gloved right hand, he picked up a marble base tennis trophy from a nearby shelf. Two steps forward, raised his right arm, and SMACK. James Mergan stretched out full length on the floor. Harry dropped to one knee and felt for a pulse.

Uh-oh. No pulse.

Now what? He hadn't meant for this to happen, he'd only wanted to put the guy back to sleep like everybody was supposed to be at this time of night. The way it looked now, if he got caught, the charges would quickly bump up from burglary to murder. In this state, that made him eligible for... He really didn't want to think about that part. Time to do something quick. One of the other house guests might've heard the commotion. At least he'd had the leather driving gloves on during all this.

Dropping the tennis trophy onto the floor, Harry raced to the safe, grabbed both stacks of money and stuffed them into his robe pockets. At the doorway to the study, he leaned out into the foyer and listened. No one appeared to be stirring.

Barely touching the carpet with his slippered feet, Harry dashed up the stairs and down the hall. He stopped one door short of the bedroom he was supposed to be sleeping in. If he hid the money behind the dresser in Johnston's bedroom and the police found it there, then Johnston would take the blame. And, if the police didn't find the money, then Harry could always retrieve it for himself later. He started formulating a plan to keep himself out of trouble.

Five minutes later, the money was safely hidden, Johnston appeared to still be asleep and Harry was back down in the study. He glanced carefully around the room at the safe, the painting, the tennis trophy, the dead home owner. Had he left any evidence which incriminated him? Nope, didn't look like it.

Now, if he called the police himself and claimed he found the body, then he could stick around and keep track of anything which pointed the finger of guilt in his direction. And maybe he could even point the finger in someone else's direction. Yeah, that's what he would do.

Going to the mahogany desk, Harry picked up the phone and punched in 9-1-1. Putting a touch of frantic emotion into his voice, Harry told a story about hearing a noise, going downstairs and finding the recently deceased. Yes, he was calling from the owner's study.

And, oh yeah, the safe was open. No, he didn't know if anything was stolen. And, yes, he would stick around until the police showed up. No, he wouldn't touch anything.

Harry hung up the phone. Had he forgotten anything? He took another quick look around. Oh yeah, the gloves. He couldn't very well meet the police with his leather driving gloves still on. Once more, he dashed up the stairs. This time, he went to his own bedroom. No blood stains on the gloves, so he stuffed them in the bottom of his suitcase and closed the lid.

Hearing sirens in the distance, Harry ran back down the stairs and composed himself to meet the police.

QUESTION: You are the homicide detective. You responded to the crime scene within a half hour after the 911 call and took a statement from Harry. The evidence techs have dusted the entire study for fingerprints and gathered up the evidence. Now, you have all the reports and evidence in front of you. What mistake did Harry make?

SOLUTION: Harry forgot to take his gloves off when he called the police. If he were an innocent witness, then his fingerprints should have been found on the telephone receiver and number buttons ...but they weren't.

SOMEONE'S INSIDE

Kate placed the last of her folded clothes neatly into the suitcase and lowered the lid. Had anything been forgotten? She made one last check: sandals, clothes, swimsuit, airline tickets, passport. Seemed like these days you needed a passport just to go out of the country, even to Mexico for a week. Well, everything seemed to be in proper order.

Pulling the zipper closed on the soft-sided luggage, she then tugged the suitcase upright and carried it out of the bedroom and into the hall. So many things to do before catching a cab to the airport: e-mails to check, appliances to unplug, put the newspaper on hold, be sure all doors and windows were locked. The check list went on and on, but then that was the way her busy life had been going lately. She definitely needed this vacation.

Down the stairs and depositing her suitcase at the front door, Kate noticed that the lock in the door handle was set, but the deadbolt wasn't thrown. Only now, she couldn't remember whether or not she'd set the deadbolt when her mother left the house a couple of hours earlier this morning after having coffee. Normally, Kate wouldn't dwell on this type of oversight for very long, but the six o'clock news these days was awful. The TV kept blaring out stories of home invasions, scams and identity theft in nearby city neighborhoods, so Kate had been taking extra precautions lately to avoid falling victim to any of these problems. She locked the deadbolt.

Moving on to the kitchen, Kate unplugged the toaster and the coffee pot, checked all the windows and the back door. She paused at the sink. Water dripped slowly from the faucet, one pinging drop after the other. She turned the handle tighter. The dripping stopped. Then there was the abandoned water glass next to the faucet and a smeared butter knife lying on the counter.

"You'd think my mom would put her used dishes in the dish washer," she almost whispered. In a matter of seconds, both objects were placed in the wash racks and the appliance door firmly closed.

In the resulting silence, Kate heard the creaking of a floorboard upstairs. She raised her eyes and muttered something about old houses and cold weather.

Hurrying through the living room, she noticed the scuffs in the carpet nap and a couple of dark stains in the beige material. Time to shampoo the rug, she thought, but not now. It would have to wait until her return. That was one more item for her future list.

To save herself a little time this morning, Kate put on her winter jacket before walking down the main floor hall and into the study. En route, she tried to think of anything else on her leaving home list that needed doing before her departure.

In the study, one of the twin, accordion-type,

louvered doors to the study's closet appeared to be partially ajar. She gently pushed the door shut as she passed by on her way to the computer.

Walking around the desk, Kate plopped down into the leather office chair and scooted the chair up to the computer keyboard. She'd do a quick check of her e-mails, then power down the computer to help protect all her personal and business files. As she reached for the mouse, she noticed two stray paper clips, a ball point pen at the foot of the monitor, plus the multiple stacks of loose paper on the desktop.

"I really do need to clean this up," she reminded herself. Then she clicked on her e-mail.

It was while wriggling around on the warm leather cushions of her office chair, trying to get more comfortable, that the realization came to Kate. She sat perfectly still and listened. There were no troubling sounds which couldn't be explained, but someone was in the house. She was positive. Out of the corner of her eye, she watched the closet door and wondered.

Picking up her cell phone, Kate punched in 911 and provided the emergency operator with the necessary name and address, all the while pretending that she was placing a temporary hold on the newspaper until vacation was over. When the operator stated this was a police line and not a place to cancel the newspaper, Kate replied, "I know that." The operator quickly caught on that something was wrong and Kate couldn't speak freely about her situation.

Making the out loud excuse she had to find her newspaper account number to ensure she got credit for the missed newspapers, Kate left the study, hurried down the hallway, out the front door and across the street to her neighbor's house until police could arrive.

QUESTION: How did Kate know someone was inside her house?

SOLUTION: When Kate sat in her leather office chair, she noticed the cushions were warm. The intruder had sat in the chair long enough, while browsing through her computer files looking for identity information to steal, that Kate was able to feel his body warmth remaining in the leather cushions. And, since the body warmth was still there, the thief hadn't had time to go far.

FLEA MARKET TREASURE

I n his excitement, Oscar let the screen door slam shut behind him. "Mabel, wait until you see what I found this time," he hollered as he entered the kitchen. "I had to do some talking, but it's a steal, and I got it for only three hundred dollars."

Mabel, his wife of forty plus years, straightened up from sliding a casserole dish into the oven. She figured she had pretty well seen all the ups and downs of her husband's shopping for treasures at the local weekend flea market, but he did seem to be really enthused about his latest purchase, so maybe she should pay a little more attention to this one.

Breathing heavily, Oscar pulled a chair out from the kitchen table and sat down. He flopped a cloth shopping bag onto the table top and hurriedly reached inside.

"Okay," said Mable, "show me what treasure you found this time."

Removing a sturdy cardboard tube from the bag, Oscar popped a clear plastic stopper from one end, tilted the tube and slowly slid a rolled-up piece of brown-stained parchment out onto the table top. The parchment's edges were curled and frayed.

"What in the world is that?" she inquired.

"That is a valuable old letter," replied Oscar, "at least 800 years old."

"Well, that brown color could just be coffee stains to make it look that old."

"No, no," said Oscar in excitement, "you don't find writing paper like this for today's letters. Look at how it's worn on the edges, and right here's the date it was written."

"I'll take your word for that," replied Mable. "So, who wrote this old letter, and who did it go to?"

"It's from King Richard the First of England, you know, Richard the Lionheart from back in Robin Hood times. Anyway, he wrote this letter to his mother, Eleanor of Aquitaine, when the Austrians were holding him for ransom and his brother King John was paying the Austrians at the same time to keep him prisoner in their castle." Oscar shook his head. "It was a real mess of politics at that time."

Mable picked up the letter gingerly with both hands for closer inspection. A small flake of brown parchment detached itself and drifted downward.

"Be careful," said Oscar, "it's a little fragile after all those years."

"Looks to me like it's written in French."

"Yep," replied Oscar, "Richard may have been the King of England, but he didn't know much English, so he wrote in French. I know my history for that time period."

"What makes you think it was the same famous Richard who wrote it?"

Oscar pointed at the signature located at the bottom of the letter. "See right there, that's his name."

Mable looked at the scrawled words: King Richard I.

"And where did this flea market salesman say he got this old-time letter?"

"Well," said Oscar, "the man said he found it hidden in a decrepit old trunk he bought at an estate sale when he was in England touring medieval castles last year. I don't think the man realized what this letter was really worth, so I got a terrific deal on it."

"Tell me again how much did you paid for it?" asked Mable.

"Only three hundred dollars," said Oscar, "but I think it's a real valuable collector's item. Something that could belong in a museum."

Mable dropped the letter back onto the table. "Oscar," she said, "I know my history too, and I think you got taken to the cleaners this time."

QUESTION: Other than the low price, why does Mable think the flea market salesman duped Oscar into buying a fake antique letter?

SOLUTION: While it was and still is a common practice to count the heads of a dynasty and then assign what is called a Regnal number after each monarch of the same name, the First isn't designated as such until the Second comes along. Thus, the first King Richard would not have signed his name as King Richard I. The letter was an obvious forgery based on the signature alone.

end

ABOUT THE AUTHOR

R.T. Lawton is a retired federal law enforcement agent and a past member of the Board of Directors for the Mystery Writers of America. He has over 140 short stories in various publications, to include *Alfred Hitchcock Mystery Magazine*, the *Who Died in Here?* anthology, the *West Coast Crime Wave* e-anthology, *The Mystery Box* (an MWA anthology), the *Die Behind the Wheel* anthology, *Easyriders Magazine*, *Outlaw Biker Magazine* and ten mini-mysteries in *Woman's World Magazine*.

Connect with me online at
http://rtlawton.weebly.com

Discover other exciting eBook short stories by R.T. Lawton available now at Amazon Kindle Books and soon in paperback.

Title 1: 9 Deadly Tales

Title 2: 9 Historical Mysteries

Title 3: 9 Holiday Burglars

Title 4: 9 Twin Brothers Bail Bond Mysteries

Title 5: 9 Chronicles of Crime

BIBLIOGRAPHY

"Cold Facts" previously published in Woman's World magazine 12/12/2006.

"An Open and Shut Case" copyright 2012

"Caught in the Tide" copyright 2006

"It Didn't Add Up" previously published in Woman's World magazine 03/27/2007

"Come into My Parlor" copyright 2008

"Grave Trouble" copyright 2007

"Keeping Up with Inspector Jones" previously published as "Building a Case" in Woman's World magazine 01/30/2012"

In Plain View" copyright 2012

"One for the Road" copyright 2016

"Officer, It was Self-Defense" previously published in Woman's World magazine 07/19/2012

"One Step at a Time" copyright 2007

"The Almost Clever Thief" previously published as "The Not So Clever Thief" in Woman's World magazine 05/19/2011

"One Wrong Step" copyright 2006

BONUS STORY

Introduction to
A Modular Story

Short stories are usually written in two forms. The most common method is the linear form. Here, the story is told in chronological sequence from the beginning to the climax.

The second method is the nonlinear form where the story is told in scenes or modules out of sequence. This is usually known as a modular story. Here, each scene or module contains a clue or reference pertinent to the conclusion of the story. A good example from the movie sector is the film *Pulp Fiction*, starring John Travolta and Samuel L. Jackson as hitmen.

The following is my modular story, "And the Band Played On."

AND THE BAND PLAYED ON

By

R.T. Lawton

2:34, Sunday Morning

Chubbs stood by the kitchen's two swinging doors and looked out on the noisy scene before him. White gangsters with their stern-looking bodyguards had come up from the city, while black numbers runners sported their flashy women, and bootleggers paid plenty to drink their own hooch run in across the border. On the other side of the room, rival madams tried hard to ignore each other, using large feather fans to furiously move the air in front of them. A couple of known confidence men along the bar cautiously eyed the crowd for marks as local politicians shook hands and slapped the backs of financial supporters and big-time vote getters. Sprinkled throughout the prominent gathering moved wealthy businessmen and their well-dressed wives, here to see and be seen. It was Saturday night slipping into Sunday morning in the heart of Harlem and the Black Cat Club was jumping.

Having already counted his waiter's tips, Chubbs was looking forward to calling it a night and going home, crawl in bed and start sawing logs. Church services was early and he knew his ol' lady would be all over him to roll his lazy butt out of bed and get dressed. Should've never bought her that new hat, he told himself. Now she couldn't wait to show it off to all them church-going ladies down at the Harlem Gospel Church. Best Chubbs could do in that solemn place was try not to doze off if'n the preacher got longwinded in his sermon.

Right now, he wished all these sports would go home and let him get started on cleanup. Sorrowfully, he glanced down at his own evening wear. The once polished black Oxfords on his feet were looking scuffed, his neatly creased black trousers seemed to have given up their stiff edges, starting to drag a little at the heels, while his white shirt had already lost most of its starch. His waiter's white apron tied loose at his waist showed a couple of food stains from him being bumped by patrons moving past the densely packed tables while he was serving those that was already seated. And, his dogs was wore out from all the walking he'd done from the kitchen to the tables and back again. Yet, in spite of the tiredness, he occasionally found his toes tapping to the ragtime jazz being played by the lively band on stage.

It was only when he remembered how his wife always demanded an accounting of everything he did and saw on the nights he worked at the Club, with a lot of her "uh-huhs" and "I see's" coming from her mouth, that his tapping feet lost some of their energy. Yep, she was gonna give him hell again for rubbing elbows with all them sinners hanging out at the Black Cat, even though that was his job. If it wasn't for this being one of the few jobs he could get and if he didn't make so much money here, she'd surely make him quit, just to save his soul from being tempted by evil, if nothing else. Now his feet quit moving altogether and he tried not to enjoy the music. Even with one horn player missing for this last show, the band was still great.

Man, what he needed was a break, sneak out in the alley and catch a smoke.

Stepping back through one of the swinging doors, he

glanced quickly around the kitchen. With nobody paying any mind to him, Chubbs sidestepped to the back door, opened it and emerged into the alley. Out here with the door shut, the music was muted some, but he could still hear the driving beat pounding through the walls.

Moving a few feet away from the light over the door, he slid into the shadows, reached into his pants pocket under the waiter's apron and took out a pack of Camels and a wooden kitchen match. Striking his thumb across the tip of the matchhead, he leaned forward to put flame to the far end of his cigarette. It was in the flare of the burning phosphorus that he thought he saw something on the other side of the alley.

Chubbs hoped what was burned into his retinas wasn't what he thought it was, but there was only one way to find out. He stepped out into the light and approached the metal garbage cans in the half-darkness on the opposite side. And, there it was on the alley floor, partially hidden by the cans. A dress shoe with the sole facing him and the toe pointed straight up. One step closer and he made out the leg of someone slumped against the brick wall. A man dressed up for nightlife. Dull light from the bulb over the restaurant back door glistened off a pool of dark liquid puddled around the body.

He hurriedly stepped back.

"Hey, Chubbs, that you?" boomed a male voice.

At first, Chubbs thought the man slumped against the building was the one talking to him and his heart inserted an extra beat out of rhythm. Then he realized the voice came from somewhere behind him. His head snapped around to look over his left shoulder. There on the back stoop stood one of the other waiters. The closing door slowly dampened noise from inside.

"Sorry, man," said Alfred, "didn't mean to make you

jump like that." He started walking over to where Chubbs stood. "What was you studying on so hard there in them shadows by the wall?"

"I think it's a dead guy."

Alfred stopped where he was.

"You sure he's dead?"

"If'n my car engine leaked like that, I'd say its motor was surely dead. I'm gonna say the same for that fella."

Alfred backed up a step.

"You kill him?"

"Not me, he was already laying there when I came out for a smoke."

"You gonna call the cops?"

"Thinking about it."

Alfred took another step back and half turned for the door.

"Wouldn't make that call if I was you."

"Why not?"

By now, Alfred was on the back stoop, reaching for the door handle.

"Cuz if you did kill that man, then you best run to save your skin. And if you didn't kill him, the cops are gonna blame you anyway as the person on the scene."

"Told you, I didn't do it."

"Don't matter. You'd be spending the rest of the night in a downtown cell, sweating under a hot spot light with them mens and their rubber hoses."

Now, Chubbs took a few steps away from the body.

"You may be right."

Alfred opened the back door.

"Damn right, I'm right."

He stepped inside and left the door open.

"And another thing," said Alfred, "I didn't see nothing. In fact, I was never even in this alley tonight or any other night."

Chubbs moved quickly to the back stoop and grabbed the door handle before the door could close.

"I hear you," said Chubbs. "You just taken the words right outta my mouth."

Chubbs shut the door behind him. Far as he was concerned, he was safer inside with the crowd of sinners.

11:15, Saturday Evening, main room

Three table rows back from the dance floor, and at a small table up against the right side-wall of the Black Cat Club, the waiter set two drinks down on the white tablecloth and asked if there would be anything more. Giuseppe Gravioni, also referred to in some circles as Joey the Juice, waved the waiter away. Then, Joey waited until the nightclub employee was out of hearing before leaning forward to continue his conversation with the slender hood known as Rico, sitting on the other side of the table.

"I got this thing going with the band's lead singer," Joey explained. He nodded towards the dance floor where a tall female on stage just beyond the open space was crooning a blues song into a large microphone.

Rico picked a piece of lint off the sleeve of his pinstriped suit and swiveled his head to take a look. What he saw was a slinky black dress that did nothing to hide the singer's full curves, nice legs from what he could glimpse, a pretty face in light tan tones and long black hair hanging over her shoulders. He wondered at the time if her hair had been straightened, but that wasn't really his business. To each his own.

"Nothing should happen in front of her," said Joey.

"I understand," replied Rico as he returned his attention to the Sicilian across from him.

"This being my club," Joey said, "everybody works for

me, so what I say goes."

Rico nodded in agreement.

"But," continued Joey, "I got this little problem with one of the horn players."

Rico swiveled his head again to peer at the stage. There were two trumpet players, both dressed in black tuxedos, white shirts and red cummerbunds.

"The light-skinned one on the right," said Joey. "He's first horn or first seat or whatever them guys call it. I told him to lay off the singer, but I hear tell he's still sniffing around. Me telling him once shoulda been enough. Maybe he don't listen so good, so now I'm gonna to let you solve my little problem. Out in the alley would be nice, maybe when the band takes a break."

"Leave it to me. After tonight, you won't see him no more."

"One more thing," said Joey.

Rico raised his left eyebrow.

"I hear you're good with a knife."

"That's the rumor going 'round."

"So, make this guy suffer. And make it messy. People need to understand the message I'm sending."

"Consider it done."

Rico scooted back his chair and got up from the table. He went over to sit at the bar where he had a good view of the two horn players. Turned out, he had to wait through another full session before his man went outside for a break.

11:50, Saturday Evening, backstage

Francine sat in front of her makeup table and looked at Mindy, the backup singer, reflected beside her in the mirror.

"I'm a little bit scared and don't know which way to

go," she admitted.

Mindy gave a low throated chuckle.

"Oh honey, with your looks and talent, you can always find another horn player, but how often does a girl get the chance to land a big nightclub owner. So what if he's an Italian gangster, that just adds to the excitement of the romance."

"But, I don't love Joey. My heart only seems to come alive when I'm around Marcel."

"Girl, that Mister Joey will dress your body up in the best clothes and he'll place expensive jewelry on your fingers and around your pretty neck. That man will take care of you like you've never been taken care of in your life."

Francine bobbed her head towards the mirror.

"I know that, but Marcel..."

"What can Marcel give you?" countered Mindy. "He's good, but he'll never be more than just a trumpet player in a jazz band. So, look at your other choice. With all his money, Mister Joey can also take your singing career all the way to the top."

"I'm not so sure of that," replied Francine. "Joey is more of the possessive type. I think he'd keep me here in his night club like a canary in a cage."

"That would be one hell of a sweet cage," said Mindy. "I could live that way."

Francine took that moment to dab the powder puff on her cheeks and throat before altering the conversation slightly.

"You know," she said, "if I go somewhere else with Marcel that leaves the lead singer position open. You could always step up and take my place. Maybe the gilded cage could be your dream."

Mindy shook her head.

"Mister Joey don't look at me the way he looks at you. And, I know for a fact that he's already told Marcel to stay away from you, so you'd better make up your mind fast before something bad happens."

"Marcel wants me to go south with him, someplace way out of state. Says he'll tell me all about it when the band takes a break after the midnight set. I'm supposed to meet him in the alley out back."

"Your big break is right here in the big city, girl. Choose wisely."

Francine was about to answer, when the dressing room door opened and the cigarette girl came in. She walked over behind Francine and spoke towards the lead singer's image in the mirror.

"Mister Gravioni says he'd like to see you at his table right after the midnight show. Said to come straight over from the stage."

Francine finished applying her bright red lipstick.

"Tell him I'll be there."

The girl started to leave, but Francine grabbed her arm.

"Wait a minute, please. Would you take a message to Marcel for me? I won't have a chance to talk to him until after I meet with Joey."

"Okay, but hurry. I have to get back on the floor. These cigarettes don't sell themselves."

Quickly, Francine scrawled a note on a piece of paper, explaining to Marcel that she wanted to hear what he had to say, but she would be late meeting him in the alley. At the bottom of the paper, she added a warning for Marcel to be careful, that Joey was making noises about finding a new horn player for the band. Then, she folded the note and handed it to the cigarette girl.

"Give this only to Marcel. Make sure nobody else gets it."

"I understand."

Francine turned back to the mirror, fluffing her hair to get ready for the band's midnight set.

Mindy waited until the cigarette girl was out the door before speaking again.

"You still don't know what you're doing, do you girl?"

3:45, Sunday Morning, the alley

Two Homicide Detectives from the Harlem precinct stood by the overflowing trash cans in the alley behind the night club and looked down at the body.

"What you think, John?"

Big John Jackson played the beam of his flashlight over the dead man's face.

"I think he pissed somebody off. The man's got one hell of a second smile under his chin. Bad enough to bleed him out."

Detective Thomas Jones hunkered down over the body to get a better view at the damage, then moved back a little so as not to get anything on his shoes. Wouldn't look good if the police photographer got photos of shoe prints in the victim's blood, shoe prints that didn't belong to the killer.

"Damn near earlobe to earlobe," said Thomas. "Looks like the killer sliced him with something a surgeon would use. That's the only wound I see up top."

"Check his hands," said John. "He's got a deep cut on the back of his right one. Don't appear to be nothing anywhere else."

As directed, Thomas carefully inspected both hands.

"Strange," he said. "Defensive wounds are usually on the palms, not on the back of the hands."

"Maybe he raised it at the last moment to protect his throat."

"Maybe. But that don't feel right to me. We'll see what the coroner says when he gets here."

Big John let that go and moved his flashlight beam slowly up and down on the right side of the body. He stopped when he saw an object laying in the pool of dark red liquid.

"What'd you find?" asked the other detective.

"Looks like a switchblade to me," John answered.

"Think it's the murder weapon?"

"Could be, if it's sharp enough to cut like that."

Detective Jones studied the open-bladed knife pinned in the flashlight beam.

"So maybe the killer did his thing, then threw the knife down by the body so he wouldn't be caught with the murder weapon on him?"

"Looks like it."

Detective Jackson started to say something more, but then glanced up as the Precinct Captain came striding down the alley with one of the shift Lieutenants.

"Brass is here," Jackson whispered to his partner.

"What have you boys got?" asked the Captain when he came to a stop a few feet away.

Jackson stiffened. But Jones put a quieting hand on his shoulder and took over the talking, explaining what they had determined so far, starting with an anonymous phone call about a body.

"Find a hat in the alley?" inquired the Captain.

"No sir," said Jones.

"That probably means the victim came from inside the night club," stated the Captain, "and his hat's still with the hat check girl. Find anything else out here?"

"Some cigarette butts here and there. Might be something, might not. Could just be a popular spot for club employees to take a break."

138

"So then one of them should know something," ventured the Lieutenant.

The Captain glared at both detectives.

"Better get on it while all them people are still here. I want this taken care of before I have my morning coffee."

He glanced at his watch for emphasis.

"Sure thing, Cap'n."

Big John nodded his agreement but managed to keep his mouth shut for now.

"We'd better line up all the employees," said Jones in a low voice to Jackson as they headed for the back door of the Black Cat Club. "Put the fear of God into them people one at a time someplace private where we can work on them. Hope for a break on this killing. Get the Captain off our back quick. Seems he's always harping how bad it looks for the precinct whenever these solid citizens get murdered up here in our neighborhood."

"If them so-called solid citizens stayed in their own part of the city instead of coming up here to savor their vices," Detective Jackson muttered, "then neither side would have these kinds of problems. Let's go see if somebody can identify him."

11:55, Saturday Evening into Sunday, main room

Peg carried the wooden tray that was supported around her neck with a soft leather strap. She'd refilled the empty spaces in the tray with the most popular brands of cigarettes, cigars, candy and chewing gum. Sell the customers what they wanted, and maybe a little flirting with the males to get bigger tips. Make the guys feel like they were somebody, at least for tonight. The short skirts the owner made his cigarette girls wear with their high heels, silk hose and lowcut blouses didn't hurt business at all, made the men even more generous about handing over the cash.

As soon as she'd left the jazz singer's dressing room on her way to deliver the note to Marcel, she'd run into the nightclub manager. He motioned her to come over where he stood.

"Where you been?"

"I had to run an errand."

He grabbed her arm above the elbow and squeezed.

"You're supposed to be on the floor, working, not running personal errands."

"The errand wasn't for me, it was for Mister Gravioni. He told me to deliver a message for him to the lead jazz singer, so I did."

The manager dropped his hand from her arm and looked around to see if anybody important was watching.

"Then go on about your business."

He walked off as if he had concerns elsewhere.

Peg tucked the folded note from Francine to Marcel under one of the packs of cigarettes in her tray. No way could she deliver it now. The band members were already coming back onto the stage, so the note would have to wait until they took another break. And even then, she wasn't too happy about being a messenger girl for the band. That didn't make her any money, but it could definitely get her in trouble with management.

For the next hour or so, Peg made her way through the tables of patrons and along the long wood and shiny brass bar on the left side of the main room. Wherever a customer thought he needed something she had, that's where she went. Twice, she returned to the back room and refilled her tray. Each time, management checked what stock she took to ensure the inventory count came out right for the end of night.

It was while refilling her tray this last time that she

noticed the note was no longer in the bottom of the tray. Carefully, she picked up each item in her flat wooden box to see if the note had slid under one of the other items. No luck. The piece of paper must've slipped out when she was making a sale and she didn't notice.

"Lose something?"

Peg glanced up to see the manager watching her.

"Thought I had an extra dollar bill tucked in here somewhere. Guess I was wrong."

"You lose money, that's your problem. You still owe us for what you sold and for any stuff you don't turn in at end of shift."

Peg gave him her best customer smile.

"No problem."

Then, she turned away, headed back to the floor.

At the other end of the room, she saw the band members stepping off the stage, going on break. Marcel, trumpet case in hand, was making his way for the kitchen's swinging doors. No doubt headed for the alley.

Well, she didn't have the note to give him, so there wasn't much she could tell him, just have to let it go. These people would have to work out their own problems for themselves, without her.

She turned towards the bar and put her customer smile back on when a man called out for cigarettes.

After all, she had to make a living.

11:45, Saturday Evening, men's dressing room

"So whatcha gonna do?"

Marcel took a silver flask out of the inside pocket of his tuxedo jacket and unscrewed the metal cap. He took a long drink of whiskey and handed the flask to Lionel, the other trumpet player.

Lionel took a short taste and handed back the flask.

Marcel left the top off.

Both horn players kept their voices low so the other band members wouldn't overhear them in the crowded men's dressing room. The air had the slight smell of sweat, stale cigarette smoke and sweet bourbon.

"Anyways you look at it," Marcel said, "it's time for me to move on. I told Francine to meet me in the alley at the next break and we'd discuss the situation."

"Think she'll go with you?"

Marcel took another pull from the flask.

"Don't know, but hope so."

"Best take it easy with that whiskey, Marcel. You'll ruin your lip for playing tonight."

Marcel gave a half smile and shrugged his shoulders.

"Don't matter. I'm leaving shortly after I speak to Francine when the midnight show is done. She comes with me or she don't. And, if she don't show up, then there's my answer. Either way, I'm still gone."

"Where you headed? Chicago?"

"Nope, that city's too close to New York. Joey's probably got connections I don't want to run into working in Chicago."

"Then where?"

"I'm thinking New Orleans. Hear tell they've got a hot jazz scene going on down there. Somebody will need a good horn player. And, with Francine's voice, it won't be no problem to get her a job as a singer if she comes along."

"So, I won't be seeing you after this next show we about to do?"

Marcel shook his head and stuck out his hand.

Lionel clasped him on the shoulder with one hand and shook his proffered hand with the other.

"We had some good times, played some good music

together. I'm going to miss you."

"Miss you too, Lionel."

Lionel stood up and adjusted his tuxedo.

"We'd best be getting on stage, got this one last show to do together."

Marcel took another drink from his flask, screwed the cap back on and put the flask in his jacket pocket. Then he too stood up.

"You be careful out there," said Lionel. "Keep your eyes open until you're well out of town."

"Don't worry about me," replied Marcel. He patted the side of his red cummerbund. "I keep my protection right here. Her name's Maybelline and she's the sharpest straight razor a man ever called his own. She slices finer than a frog hair."

Lionel gave an encouraging grin.

Then the two of them headed for the dressing room door to do Marcel's last show at the Black Cat Club in Harlem.

end

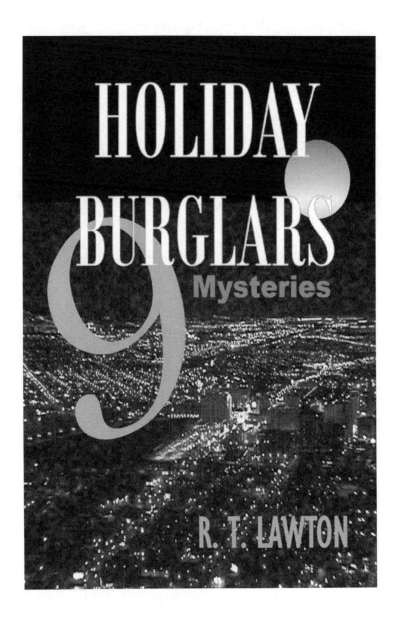

BLACK FRIDAY

It was the Friday after Thanksgiving and Yarnell knew he was in trouble as soon as the pawn shop door swung shut behind him and he saw Lebanese George standing with both hands stretched towards the ceiling. It sure as hell didn't look to him like George was in the process of changing any overhead light bulbs. If what was going on was what Yarnell thought it was, he was pretty sure that professional courtesy between criminals didn't necessarily get extended to off-duty burglars during a stick-up. Immediately taking one giant step to the rear, Yarnell reached behind his back with his right hand and tried to find the door knob.

Unfortunately, the jingling bell over the door must've already alerted the robber, because the young man standing to one side of the pawn shop owner quickly turned and pointed his gun in Yarnell's direction.

"Not so fast," said the robber.

Yarnell wasn't sure if that meant he was now supposed to move in slow motion or not at all, so to be on the safe side, he quit moving altogether. In fact, he thought it best under these circumstances to have his brain check to see if his lungs were still pumping air.

"Looking good," said the robber. "So how about you move this direction away from the door." He made a come-hither motion with all four fingers of his free hand.

Yarnell took two baby steps forward.

"We're getting this all worked out," said the robber. "Now put your hands up."

With a serious expression on his face, Yarnell raised his hands to shoulder level before venturing an opinion.

"I don't think that's a good idea."

"Why not?" asked the robber.

"Because some passerby on the sidewalk out front might see me standing here with my hands raised and then call it in as a robbery in progress."

"He's right, you know," Lebanese George chimed in as his own elbows started to sag and both hands declined a few inches from their upright position. "Like he said, any passerby could look in and see him with his hands in the air. Might cause some problems."

The robber swung his gun back towards the owner standing behind the counter.

"Get your hands up where they belong."

George stretched for the ceiling again. "Well, I don't suppose anyone can see me all the way back here, so that's probably all right," he agreed.

"Shut up," ordered the robber.

"May I say something?" Yarnell inquired.

At the sound of Yarnell's voice, the robber spun back to cover him with the pistol. A drop of perspiration slowly rolled down the robber's nose and hung on the very tip.

"What?" he practically shouted, then seemed to recover himself. "And get your hands down. We don't need no cops running in here."

Yarnell did as he was told.

"Well?" asked the robber.

"Well, what?" Yarnell asked back.

"What were you going to say?"

Yarnell reached his right hand up to scratch the top of his head. His left hand went up to remove his hat in preparation for the scratch.

"I forgot."

"Get your hands back down," ordered the robber.

"Sorry," said Yarnell as he dropped his hands again.

"Did it have anything to do with the robbery?" asked George from behind the counter. "I mean what you were going to say?"

The robber turned quickly, swinging the gun from one man to the other as if not sure which one to point it at. That single drop of perspiration suspended on the tip of his nose now became dislodged in the sudden twisting back and forth, spun off into mid-air and arced its way towards the floor. Another drop quickly rolled down to the tip and replaced it.

"Oh yeah, thanks," said Yarnell. "I remember now."

The robber cocked his head as if he could barely wait to hear what came next.

"I assume you're only taking the money," Yarnell said.

"No," piped up George from the rear of the store. "He's also stealing the higher-priced jewelry."

"He didn't get my wife's wedding ring, did he?"

"As a matter of fact, he did."

This latest exchange had the robber's head going left and right like he was watching a spirited match of ping pong. The gun had trouble keeping up.

"That won't do," said Yarnell. "That won't do at all."

"Stop it," screamed the robber. "Both of you."

"My arms are getting tired," said the owner. "I don't know how much longer I can hold them up this high."

"Get them back up there," commanded the robber as he pointed the gun at the owner again.

In the ensuing silence, the next tinkling of the little bell over the pawn shop door seemed inordinately loud. All heads inside the store swiveled toward the front doorway.

Beaumont stepped into the shop and the door closed behind him.

"C'mon, Yarnell," he said in a rush, "we gotta go look at a safe. Time's a wasting."

"You go ahead," said Yarnell without looking directly at him. "I'll be along in a little bit."

"He's not going anywhere," screamed the robber, "until I say he does."

"What's this?" inquired Beaumont.

"This is a holdup," said the robber.

Beaumont immediately raised his hands towards the ceiling.

"Get your hands down," screamed the robber.

Beaumont's hands came down to shoulder height, palms out.

"What kinda robbery is it," he asked, "where you don't put your hands up?"

"Give him a little slack," said Yarnell. "I don't think he's done this before."

"I agree," said George who by now was perched on a high stool behind the counter and only had one hand in the air. The other hand was busy raising a half-filled coffee cup to his blubbery lips.

"He doesn't seem to have much experience in this type of business," George added between slurps.

"I've had plenty of experience," exclaimed the robber as his head swiveled from the two men at the front of the store to the owner behind the counter and back again. The gun now seemed to move in the opposite direction of wherever he was looking.

"Oh yeah," replied Beaumont, "name one big job you did."

"I did the coffee shop two blocks over."

"According to what the coffee shop manager told me," said Yarnell, "the stickup man only got sixty-two bucks for that one. I'm not sure that qualifies as big."

"Well, I also did that bar up on Fifty-Third Street off the Square," said the robber. "That was a lot more than sixty-two dollars."

"Wait a minute," said Beaumont. "Isn't that the Russian bar?"

"Right," said Yarnell.

"Oh," breathed the shop owner.

"What?" asked the robber.

Beaumont sadly shook his head.

"I'm pretty sure the Russian mafia owns that bar."

"They can get pretty ruthless," added Yarnell.

"I wouldn't want to be you," said George. "You might want to leave town."

"Not with my wife's ring, he's not," said Yarnell.

"Wait a minute," said Beaumont. "You pawned Marge's wedding ring to Lebanese George here?"

"Not exactly," replied Yarnell.

"Explain not exactly."

"Well," said Yarnell, "Marge inadvertently banged her ring against the sink while doing dishes a couple nights ago and was afraid the diamond might come loose. She wanted the prongs checked to see if they were still holding tight."

"I'm listening," said Beaumont.

"Regular jewelers cost too much just to check

something like that," continued Yarnell, "but George here said he'd check the prongs out for a low, low price just cuz it was me."

"He's a good customer," said George giving a one-eyed wink to Beaumont. "He brings me some of the stuff you guys get from your night work."

"Go on," said Beaumont trying to ignore George and his comment.

"I was a little short of cash at the time...you know, for turkey, cranberries, that kinda thing...so I asked George to go ahead and borrow me some money while we was at it and I'd pay everything off when I came back. And here I am."

"You hocked your wife's wedding ring to Lebanese George," said Beaumont. He shook his head. "I sure hope Marge don't find out what you did."

"She won't be hearing it from me," said Yarnell.

"Hold on," interjected the robber. "You got cash in your pocket? I mean you're coming in to pay off the ring, right?"

It got quiet in the pawn shop.

"I'm not giving the money to you," said Yarnell. "It's to pay off my bill here with George."

The robber stuck out his left palm. "Hand over the cash."

Yarnell reached in his pocket and pulled out a wad of twenties. "Okay, but I'm not giving it to you. I'm turning it over to George here to pay my bill. What you guys do after that is between you two."

"Fine," said the robber, "pay your bill and then I'll continue robbing him."

By now, Lebanese George had both hands down to the level of the pawn shop counter. The coffee cup was empty.

"No way," said George, "you want the money, take it from him." He pointed a thick finger at Yarnell. "Under the circumstances, I don't accept payment. Your wife's ring is still in hock."

"No, it's not," replied Yarnell. "The ring is no longer in your possession. This idiot has it in his robbery bag."

"Careful," said the robber, "that's me you're talking about."

To read the rest of the story and eight more, get *9 Holiday Burglars Mysteries by R.T. Lawton*

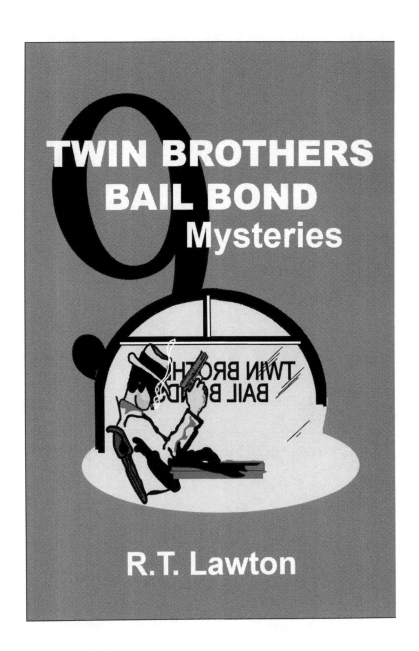

THE BOND THAT KEEPS

W ith pale stubby, almost webbed fingers, Theodore slid his business card across the grey metal table in the interview room of the San Mateo County Jail. The card read:

> TWIN BROTHERS BAIL BONDS
> Cletis Johnston, proprietor
> "When no one else will go your bond,
> we'll do you."
> Bail Agent: Theodore Oscar Alan Dewey

Jack Niedekker flipped the card over, then turned it back to the front side.

"There's no address nor phone number on this card."

"We ain't in the yellow pages either," Theodore added.

"Never heard of you guys."

Theodore mopped his balding head and bumpy face with a large white handkerchief. New, persistent beads of moisture popped out just above the well-manicured, pencil thin mustache on his upper lip, gathered at his chin and dripped down onto an oversized gold chain resting on his hairy, open shirt chest. Having to wear a sport coat in the jail when the air conditioning had crashed didn't seem to help matters.

"That's cuz we only handle special clients."

"What makes me so special?"

As Theodore's hand paused in midair, the white on white silk handkerchief dangled from his clutching fist while the left little finger on his hand pointed straight out as if it had once been broken and then improperly set. A glint of light sparkled on the errant finger from the lump of a two-carat yellow diamond set in a gold pinky ring.

"First off, Jack..."

"Hey, Bud, we don't know each other that well. Maybe you best call me Mr. Niedekker."

"Of course, *Mr. Niedekker*. In any case, you've been charged with the armed robbery of Feingold's Jewelry Store. Whereas the police don't like to mention the amount taken — it allegedly encourages others to commit similar crimes on jewelry stores —insiders have calculated the retail value at well over a million dollars. That alone, puts you in a class of your own, wouldn't you say?"

"Hey, the cops didn't catch me with any jewelry and I'm not admitting to nothing."

Theodore's two bulbous eyes stared directly into the face of their future client.

"We are not your father confessor, we are merely your bonding company. All that the two of us need to do is come together on a mutually satisfying arrangement. I have two sets of papers here for you to sign."

"Not so fast, Slick. You gave a first reason. What's the second reason for you to bond me out?"

Theodore's heavy-lidded eyes blinked.

"Mr. Niedekker, I remind you of our company's motto; 'When no one else will go your bail, we'll do you.' And believe me, with your prior record, no other bondsman will put up the large amount necessary for your bail. Seems you've been a very bad boy. You skipped bond on your last two arrests. Not really conducive to trust, is it?"

"How do you know I won't run on you guys?"

"That's where our agreement comes in."

Theodore placed the paperwork on the table so Niedekker could read both sets.

"The contract on your right is the official paperwork which will be filed with the court. It specifies a certain amount of money that you pay us to go your bond. Of course, in reality you do not pay us that amount of money. We do this simply as a sham to satisfy the court that all is on the up and up."

"I'm not sure I understand the sham part, but I don't have this kind of money on hand anyway."

"That's where the second contract, our gentlemen's agreement under the table so to speak, comes in. Here, you agree to provide a named item in your possession as security to our company, plus..."

"What item is that?"

Theodore referred to a small black notebook, flipping the pages until he found the desired reference.

"Through various channels that we won't go into, it has come to the attention of our company's proprietor that you have two specific paintings. Place them in our keeping and they will serve as warranty for your future appearance in court."

"Hey, I got lots of paintings hanging on my apartment walls, but none of them are worth more than a couple thousand dollars each. Which ones do you want?"

Theodore again referred to the black notebook.

"Not the ones on open display, *Mr. Niedekker.* We want the two you have hanging in the concealed room, the double locked vault where you hold the fruits of your nighttime endeavors. I believe they are named *Hijo de la Revolucion* and *La Angustia de Guerra.* Their combined value runs right at half a million dollars."

"How would you possibly know about those?"

"According to our sources, you committed a theft for order from a Beverly Hills fine arts gallery on Rodeo Drive, leaving much more valuable paintings behind. The local newspapers called it a meticulously planned and well-executed theft. Rather a nice move for your underworld reputation, I take it."

The room grew in silence. Loud ticking came from the clock above the door. Water knocked and gurgled in the pipes inside the walls. Somewhere down the hall, a telephone rang. Finally, Theodore cleared his throat.

"*Mr. Niedekker,* I realize that this revelation of your secrets, supposedly known only to you, comes as somewhat of a shock, but I need remind you that time is of the essence here."

Theodore began ticking off selling points on the tips of his fat little fingers, starting with the thumb.

"One, you were paid twenty-five percent up front to steal the paintings. Two, you stole the paintings. Three, you have not yet delivered the paintings to your client and won't until next month as agreed upon by both parties. Four, if our company holds the paintings temporarily as collateral, it will guarantee your court appearance, because we both know that your client is the head of a large criminal organization that as a matter of honor would have to make a messy example of you if you failed to deliver said paintings as required."

Now Theodore came to the tip of his errant little finger with the diamond pinky ring.

"Lastly, and very important to you, if you don't get bonded out, you run the risk of someone else accidentally finding where you stashed the jewels from the Feingold robbery."

With a certain wariness showing in his eyes, Niedekker folded his arms across his chest and cocked his head to one side.

"I know you won't tell me where you got your other information from, but who said I had the jewels?"

Theodore came as close as he ever did to smiling these days.

"Your partner in crime, Mr. Harvey Lightfoot, is also about to become one of our clients. Harvey, -- he allows me to call him by his first name – is a man of fire and ice, two rather interesting contrasts. I would say, a very volatile man for his line of work. He has the ability to invoke both the emotions of paranoia and hot passion to work himself up to violent acts, and then is able to use the coldness of his mind to see the action through no matter what. Which explains his priors for homicide, which somehow always seem to get bargained down to manslaughter."

"Harvey ratted me out?"

"No, no, but he did pass our polygraph exam about not leaving the store with the jewels in his possession. And since there were only two of you, that means you carried off the jewels."

"What difference does that make?"

"According to the terms of our unofficial contract, you give the paintings into our custody, plus ten percent of the jewels. Consider it a tithe. I will accompany you after your release from this institution to ensure that our company gets their fair share of the merchandise. So, if you'll just sign here and here..."

Theodore handed over a 14K gold ballpoint pen.

"...then we can get the ball rolling."

Pen in hand, Niedekker paused as if contemplating his options.

"Let's say I make arrangements for my girlfriend to turn over the paintings to your custody."

"Okay."

"It's only temporary, right? I get the paintings back after my court appearance?"

"Of course, or you may choose to repay the twenty-five percent up front commission to your patron of the stolen arts — assuming that he will accept those conditions — and go about your merry way to parts unknown."

"I see. But regardless of those circumstances, you go with me to recover the jewels so you can get your blood-out-of-the-turnip money."

"Our company doesn't like to use such terms as blood money, but essentially you are correct."

Niedekker poised with the pen over the official contract for a couple more minutes, then appeared to make up his mind. He signed at the bottom and pushed the papers across the table. He hesitated again over the signature line of the unofficial document.

Theodore turned his wrist to consult his gaudy Rolex watch, spelled with two L's, and tapped the face of the dial to signify to Niedekker that time was short.

With apparent reluctance, Niedekker signed.

Both contracts safely tucked away, Theodore continued.

"Well, *Jack*, now that we know each other better, you can show me on a map, the route you took from the jewelry store so my boss, who has excellent high level contacts within the police department, can ensure that the law will not stumble over us during the recovery process."

"Wait a minute. How do I know your guys won't gang up on me when I point out the jewels?"

"Your partner, Harvey, will come with you and I, and he will be armed with a handgun to his satisfaction. Fair enough, *Jack*?"

Niedekker thought about it, then nodded. Using his forefinger, he traced his escape route on the map. Finished, he leaned back, relaxing now that the deal had been struck. Idly, he studied the business card again.

In the background came the sound of a key turning in the lock. The door opened and a uniformed guard filled the door frame.

"Times up, Gentlemen."

Niedekker stood up from the grey metal stool bolted to the floor, then stopped.

"There is one more thing I'm slightly curious about here. Your company is Twin Brothers Bail Bonds, but the card only lists one person as the proprietor. What's the story on that?"

Theodore carefully scratched his double chin.

"Cletis and Daryl Johnston were twins. Daryl was born first, so they nicknamed him 'Twin'; Cletis was second and therefore named 'Twin Brother'. Them two were so alike that close relatives had trouble telling them apart. Very competitive boys, even against each other, especially Cletis since he was second, but then they also did everything together, to include starting up the bail bond company."

"So why only one name on the card?"

Theodore mopped his brow again.

"The brothers supposedly had a falling out over how business should be conducted. According to Cletis, Daryl was so mad over the argument that he left town in the middle of the night to start his own bail bond company in another state. After that, Cletis just never bothered to change the company's name."

"Oh, so no big thing then?"

Theodore rubbed his left hand over his bald crown, his pinky finger standing straight up.

"No, no, I'm sure not. Allegedly, Daryl was just too angry to bother taking his clothes with him and no one's heard from him since, but these are subjects I've been told not to discuss in the office and I suggest you don't bring them up in front of Mr. Johnston if you get to meet him. You'll find he can be a very persuasive man about having his own way."

A thin trickle of salty drops made their way down Theodore's back as the guard took Jack Niedekker from the room.

To read the rest of the story and eight more, get *9 Twin Brothers Bail Bond Mysteries* by R.T. Lawton

Made in the
USA
Lexington, KY